'You can't po

'Why can't I?'

'Because you really want to go to bed with me.'

Laura gasped. 'That's not true.'

'Isn't it? Tell me, Beatrice, what's it like when Sam kisses you?'

Beatrice. Laura dropped her gaze and turned crimson.

'When he kisses you, does it make your heart pound as if you're running a marathon? Do you love him, Bea?'

'Yes,' she whispered. 'I do.'

'Liar,' James breathed, and hauled her into his arms. 'This is what a kiss should be like.'

Angela Devine grew up in Tasmania, surrounded by forests, mountains and wild seas, so she dislikes big cities. Before taking up writing, she worked as a teacher, librarian and university lecturer. As a young mother and Ph.D. student, she read romantic fiction for fun and later decided it would be even more fun to write it. She is married with four children, loves chocolate and Twining's teas and hates ironing. Her current hobbies are gardening, bushwalking, travelling and classical music.

Recent titles by the same author:

MISTRESS FOR HIRE
THE PERFECT MAN

SUBSTITUTE BRIDE

BY
ANGELA DEVINE

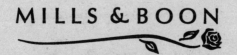

MILLS & BOON

To my daughter Sian with love.

*First published in Great Britain 1996
Harlequin Mills & Boon Limited,
Eton House, 18-24 Paradise Road, Richmond, Surrey TW9 1SR*

© Angela Devine 1996

ISBN 0 263 79933 6

*Set in Times Roman 10 on 12 pt.
01-9701-55456 C1*

*Printed and bound in Great Britain
by Mackays of Chatham PLC, Chatham*

CHAPTER ONE

'MIRROR, mirror, on the wall, should I marry Raymond Hall?'

Laura Madison gazed steadily at her own perplexed reflection and heaved a faint sigh. At twenty-nine she had begun to think of herself as a confirmed career woman, and Ray's proposal the previous evening had taken her completely by surprise. Although they had been friends for more than a year, she had never imagined that he thought of her as a possible wife.

A competent accountant, yes. A theatre companion, a tennis partner, a fellow gourmet, certainly. But someone who would share his entire life? It was unthinkable! Yet she had promised to think about it...and to give him his answer today. Her spirits sank at the prospect. As if she didn't have enough to worry about, with her sister's crazy request blurted out over the telephone only an hour ago!

Suddenly the loud toot of a car horn down below broke into her reverie. She hurried into the sitting room and hauled up the window.

'Bea!' she whispered in exasperation. 'It's only five thirty a.m. You'll wake the people in the other flats! And that's a no parking zone.'

Her younger sister grinned up at her, thrusting her long hair back off her face in a gesture that made her one of the most photographed models in Australia. Evidently Bea's mercurial spirits had taken an upward turn after her earlier gloom.

'Who cares? Anyway, you'd better hurry up or you'll be late for the airport.'

Plodding back into the hall and giving herself a final, despairing grimace in the mirror, Laura picked up her overnight bag and went downstairs.

'Now, are you clear on what you've got to do?' asked Bea, reversing out of the driveway with a squeal of tyres that made her sibling shudder.

'Yes!' retorted Laura savagely. 'I fly down to Tasmania on your plane ticket, pretending I'm you. Sam will arrive on a later plane and meet me at the real estate agent's office. Then we go and view the house together. But I still don't see the need for all this.'

'I already explained it, La-La,' said Bea, weaving in and out of the Sydney traffic, which was already heavy even at this hour. 'A wonderful house has just come on the market at a bargain price and Sam's uncle James wants to give it to us as a wedding present. But he only has a twenty-four-hour option to purchase, so we must look over it today. Except I can't fly to Tasmania myself, because I've got to go to court here in Sydney on a dangerous driving charge. It's so unfair! I wasn't driving dangerously. My foot just slipped on the accelerator and—'

'Never mind that now!' cut in Laura. 'Why don't you simply tell Uncle James that you can't come with Sam?'

'Because he already disapproves of me. I've never met him, but from what I've heard he really hates the thought of his precious nephew marrying an airhead fashion model. He's already spoken to Sam several times on the phone, trying to persuade him to call off the marriage because he thinks I'm such a fruit-loop. Too young, too irresponsible and "everyone knows that models sleep around".'

'But that's utterly unfair!' cried Laura hotly. 'Why should he condemn you when he's never even met you?'

Bea shrugged. Although she was trying to look tough, Laura saw the unmistakable flash of hurt in her dark eyes. It brought back memories of Bea at the age of five, clutching her teddy and glaring defiantly at the foster-worker who had taken them into care after their mother's death.

'Search me,' said Bea. 'It seems a bit rich considering that good old Uncle James has a reputation for seducing anything that moves, while I've only ever slept with Sam. But everyone in the Fraser family seems to dance to James's tune. Even Sam.'

'Why? What's so special about this man?' demanded Laura indignantly.

'Well, according to Sam, he's tremendously dynamic and hell-bent on having control of everything—not to mention filthy rich and dangerous to oppose. To be honest, I think Sam's very brave to insist on marrying me when James is against it. And I don't want James spoiling the wedding by becoming even more poisonous, which he will if he finds out about this dangerous driving charge. That's why you've got to cover for me!'

Laura shifted uncomfortably in her seat.

'But supposing James turns up while we're viewing the house? Won't he get a bit of a shock if Sam introduces me as his fiancée and then marries a completely different woman the weekend after this?'

Bea gave a throaty chuckle.

'Don't be such a worry-wart, Laura. James won't set eyes on you today. He's going to look at a prize bull for his beef herd and he'll be miles away. All he needs to believe is that I've shown up, as per instructions. And you're wearing my clothes and make-up, so everyone else will think you're me. What can possibly go wrong?'

Laura found out the answer to that shortly after lunchtime. It was a crisp, sunny late winter's day, with snow blanketing the dark blue mountain that loomed behind the city of Hobart and dazzling sunlight reflecting off the paler blue waters of the Derwent estuary. After an uneventful flight, a few hours' shopping and a pleasant lunch at the Sheraton, she was beginning to think her earlier fears had all been groundless. Until she went to the real estate agent's office to meet Sam.

'Hello—Miss Walters? My name is . . . Bea Madison. I'm supposed to meet my fiancé, Sam Fraser, here, and we're to view a house together.'

'Yes, of course, Miss Madison. But I'm afraid your fiancé hasn't arrived yet and I have another appointment at two o'clock. Would you mind if I take you directly to the house, and we'll leave a message for him to come and join us as soon as he gets here?'

'No, not at all,' said Laura, although she couldn't help feeling slightly taken aback. Where on earth could Sam be?

The house was enchanting, and she felt a brief pang of envy at the thought of Bea living there. Dear Bea, she was so sweet, but she would never appreciate the perfection of the glowing pink camellias in the garden, or the dark panelled entrance hall, or the gracious old sitting room with its antique furniture and its sweeping green lawns that led right down to the beachfront. Bea wasn't interested in tranquillity; she would far rather have a penthouse in the middle of Sydney's hectic King's Cross any day of the week!

Laura wandered round the house, touching the polished woodwork and thinking how much she would like to live there herself. Only her feelings of awkwardness about the situation and the occasional furtive glances that the real estate agent kept darting at her watch made her feel at all uncomfortable.

'Miss Walters, if you've got another appointment, could you leave me here to wait for Sam?' she asked at last. 'I'd be only too happy to do that. I can always...er...measure up for curtains or something while I'm waiting.'

The estate agent's face cleared.

'Well, if you're sure...'

'I'm sure. Thank you for showing me around.'

With a feeling of relief, Laura retreated into the dining room and heard the other woman's steps receding down the front path. She was just beginning to relax when the sound of a stopping car and an exchange of voices brought her senses back to full alert. One of the voices was the real estate agent's, high and twittery, but the other was deep, resonant and masculine. Laura hurried into the entrance hall with a welcoming smile on her lips.

'Sam, I'm so glad—'

She stopped in her tracks with a chill feeling of misgiving. It wasn't Bea's fiancé who stood in the doorway surveying her from under frowning dark eyebrows. In spite of his twenty-four years, Sam always seemed like a big kid to Laura, but there was no questioning that this newcomer was a fully grown man.

He was tall and powerfully built, in his mid to late thirties, with glossy dark hair and a face as arrogant and haughty as an eagle's, with the same disconcerting tawny-eyed stare. The resemblance to a bird of prey was intensified by the strong line of his nose and the pitiless, predatory curve of his mouth. Although he was dressed in conservative well-cut clothes—a camel-coloured cashmere coat worn over brown woollen trousers, a beige shirt, heather mix tie and tweed jacket—Laura couldn't control the rush of dread that overtook her at the sight of him.

A flurry of adjectives crowded into her mind to describe him, all of them inadequate. Shrewd, dangerous, demanding, unforgiving. The kind of man who made every woman in a room come on heat the moment he appeared. When he advanced on her with his hand outstretched, she flinched visibly.

'You must be Beatrice,' he said, seizing her cold fingers in a warm, crushing grip. 'I'm Sam's uncle, James Fraser.'

Her spirits plummeted, and the knowledge of her false position filled her with a hot rush of shame. In that moment her confidence ebbed away, so that she no longer felt like a grown woman and a capable accountant. Instead she was an eleven-year-old orphan with a knot of dread in her stomach and a fierce determination to protect her little sister. But how could she protect Bea now? The game was up and the only thing she could do was confess the truth.

As she looked into James Fraser's opaque golden eyes she knew with a sickening feeling that he would never forgive either of them. She should never have let Bea talk her into this ridiculous imposture!

'There's something I have to explain,' she began haltingly. 'An apology—'

'I know what you're going to say,' he cut in. 'You're going to tell me that Sam's been caught up in this

wretched airline strike so he can't join us here. Don't
worry, there's no apology needed. I know all about it.'

That was more than Laura did. She stood staring at
him in horror.

'Airline strike?' she echoed stupidly.

'Oh, hadn't you heard? The passenger planes all
around Australia have been grounded since eight o'clock
this morning. You were lucky you left Sydney when you
did. Once I heard the news on the radio I realised that
you'd be stranded down here without Sam to look after
you. Under the circumstances I decided I'd better drive
down and rescue you. If you've finished looking over
the house, I'll drive you back to my home on the east
coast and Sam can join us there as soon as he can find
transport.'

Laura blinked as the full horror of her situation began
to dawn on her.

'That's very kind of you,' she said faintly.

'Not at all. And there's no need to look as if I'm going
to bite you. My intentions are friendly, I assure you.'

As he spoke he gave her a fleeting smile which made
her feel more alarmed than ever. There was something
feral in it, mingled with an unexpected charm, so that
Laura's heart knocked against her ribs and she was left
feeling oddly breathless. Oh, Lord, that's all I need! she
thought in dismay. A case of teenage heartburn for
Wicked Uncle James.

What upset her most was the way that he was meeting
her evasive glance with an amused, mocking stare, as if
he could read her thoughts. Worse still, he seemed to
realise that she found him physically attractive and his
reaction was alarmingly blatant. His eyes narrowed as
they rested on her and he ran the tip of his tongue along
his slightly uneven white teeth, as if he were wondering

how she would taste. There was something indecently sensual in that action.

As far as James Fraser knew, she was his nephew's intended bride. So how dared he look at her as if she were something succulent to eat? Or was she imagining it? After all, was it really likely that a man as devastatingly charismatic as James Fraser would be looking at her with a gleam of naked lust in his eyes? Of course not! Now, if she really were Bea, it would be understandable. All the same, his silent, lazy scrutiny made her go hot and cold with consternation.

Fortunately she was saved from replying by the sound of the real estate agent's footsteps returning down the path. The older woman smiled at her and handed her a mobile phone.

'It's your sister, Laura, Miss Madison. She wants to speak to you. Why don't you take it into the sunroom if you want some privacy?'

Feeling slightly schizophrenic at the announcement that Laura wanted to speak to her, Laura staggered obediently into the sunroom, closed the door and slumped against it.

'Laura? This is Bea. I'm in a phone box at the court house. Listen, something awkward has happened. There's a plane strike on and Sam can't get down to Hobart to join you.'

'That's not the only awkward thing that's happened,' hissed Laura. 'Sam's Uncle James has just turned up here at the house.'

'Oh, no!' shrieked Bea. 'Does he know you're not me?'

'Shh! Keep your voice down. No, he doesn't know yet, but I'll have to tell him.'

'You can't, Laura! He'll never forgive me. He'll refuse to come to the wedding and Sam will be furious with me. Please don't tell him.'

'What else can I do?'

'Well, you could bluff it out a bit longer. Maybe we could switch places on the wedding day and he wouldn't notice.'

Laura gave a ferocious snarl of laughter.

'Be serious! You're four inches taller, twenty pounds lighter and six years younger than I am, and you have an empty space between your ears whereas I have a brain. Or I used to think I had!'

'I don't know why you're telling *me* to keep my voice down,' said Bea plaintively. 'Laura, just keep it going a bit longer. Please, please? Only until the air strike is over. Then I swear I'll come down and confess it all to him myself. After all, I'm the one to blame, aren't I? And if you tell him now he'll shout at you, instead of me. You know how you hate people shouting.'

Laura opened her mouth to argue, then gritted her teeth. Why not do exactly what Bea suggested? Let her get herself out of her hare-brained schemes for once, instead of expecting Laura to rush around setting things right for her! It would serve her right.

But that's not fair to James, protested a small voice inside her. Defiantly, Laura pushed down the niggling doubt. Let James take care of himself! He looked tough enough to cope if the truth came out. Besides, after the arrogant, unjust prejudice he had shown towards Bea, he deserved whatever he got! And if he *had* been mentally undressing Laura, he deserved to be taken down a peg or two.

Her next words surprised her just as much as they did her sister. 'All right. But you're going to owe me for this, Bea.'

She had little time to regret her rash decision, for as soon as she emerged with the telephone James instructed the real estate agent to lock up the house and hustled Laura into his gleaming silver Mercedes, which was parked outside. As the car purred north he cast her a keen sideways glance.

'How did you like the house?' he asked.

'It's lovely!'

'You think you'll be happy to live there, then?'

She flushed crimson at the unwelcome reminder that she wouldn't be the one living there in any case. This was going to be a dangerous conversation. She would have to remember that she was supposed to be Bea, with all of Bea's very different attitudes, although perhaps without quite so much of her sister's flamboyance.

'Yes, I'm sure I will,' she said in a subdued voice.

'You're not going to miss the fast-track life in Sydney too much?'

Laura hung her head and paused before answering. Privately she had worried about the same thing herself. Bea was such a pleasure-loving creature, always going out to parties and discos. It had come as a complete shock when she had fallen for the silent, rugged Sam Fraser, who was more at home on the back of a horse than on a dance-floor. But Laura had no doubts about the depths of her sister's attachment.

'I'll have Sam to help me.'

James's mouth tightened.

'Where did you meet Sam?'

'On a country property near Tamworth. He was working as a stockman there and I...I was modelling some country clothes for a photographic shoot.'

Laura held her breath, wondering whether the truth was going to come out this very moment. Surely a single glance would be enough to convince James that she wasn't tall enough or thin enough or young enough or gorgeous enough to be a fashion model? But James seemed to have no trouble at all in accepting her in that role. Perhaps it was because she had taken the precaution of wearing Bea's appalling striped cardigan over her own tan knitted trouser suit. She had also left her long dark hair hanging loose around her shoulders and made up her face with far more lipstick and eyeshadow than she normally used. The whole effect made her feel like a different woman—swashbuckling, assertive and decidedly reckless. Was this how Bea felt all the time?

'How long ago did you meet?'

'Six months.'

'Six months? That's not long to decide that you want to be married.'

Laura's eyes flashed.

'It was long enough for me.' She thought of Sam and tried to immerse herself in the feeling she knew Bea had for him, but it was no use. All Sam could ever be to her was a kind of pleasant younger brother. Perhaps the knowledge showed in her face, for she heard her voice waver unconvincingly. 'I'm in love with him.'

'Are you indeed?' James's eyebrows rose sceptically. 'Well, perhaps. But love on its own seems a rather inadequate basis for a marriage.'

There was a definite sneer in his tone now, and Laura's fighting instincts were roused.

'I don't agree with you,' she snapped. 'I think it's the most important basis there is.'

'And did you get that impression from your own family?'

She could feel her whole body tensing, as if she were a wounded animal readying itself for fight or flight, as the memories of her own unsatisfactory family came crowding back to her. How much had Sam told this hateful man about it? He must have told him something, surely? In vain she struggled to keep her voice steady.

'No, I didn't get it from my family. I don't know how much Sam has told you, but I don't have any family to speak of. Only a sister. Our parents were migrants and they split up when we were small. My mother died of cancer when I was el ... five, and my father never came back. We spent most of our childhood in foster homes.'

'I'm sorry,' he said curtly.

'So am I.'

Maybe he was genuinely sorry, but to her defensive ears something in his voice sounded disdainful, as if her background was exactly what he'd expected. Not her fault, perhaps, but nothing to be proud of either. She was shocked by the blaze of rage that filled her. How dared he sit there, making these smug judgements about her ... or Bea? Well, it served him right that they were making a fool of him!

Ordinarily she would have felt guilty and embarrassed about taking part in such a brazen deception, but James seemed to bring out the worst in her, revealing a side of her character that she had never dreamed existed. Reckless, defiant and totally deceitful. All the same, the old, familiar Laura was probably lurking somewhere in the background, all ready to give the game away by stammering and contradicting herself. Perhaps it was best to avoid conversation as much as possible?

Not wanting to be interrogated any further, she gave an exaggerated yawn and rubbed her left hand over her eyes.

'Look, if you don't mind, I might try and get some sleep; it's been a long day.'

'Of course. We still have a three-hour drive ahead of us, so that's a sensible idea.'

Through the fringe of her half-closed eyelashes, Laura saw James glance at her assessingly from time to time. Yet, in spite of the way a self-conscious flush was mounting to her cheeks, she somehow managed to keep her breathing quiet and regular. Would he discover how she had tricked him? Would he be furious when he did? Somehow the prospect of seeing James Fraser absolutely wild with rage sent a tremor of sensation through her limbs that was closer to excitement than apprehension.

Would he shout and storm around the room, grab her by the shoulders and thrust his face close to hers as he demanded an explanation? She imagined how it would feel to have those tough, masculine hands seizing her urgently and that hawk-like face so close to hers that she could see the network of tiny lines around his eyes and the way his white, even teeth gritted together...

She swallowed hard and tried to remember what Sam had told her about his uncle, but it didn't amount to much. Sam was a naturally taciturn person, and in any case Laura had not had the faintest idea that the information would ever prove important to her.

Vaguely she had the impression that Sam's family had settled in the colony of Van Diemen's Land in the very early days and that they had old money derived from the farming of merino sheep and the ownership of a woollen mill in Hobart. But about James himself she knew tantalisingly little. Only that he had taught Sam to ride and fish and had been an unsparing taskmaster when his nephew had worked on his property for two years as a stockman.

She couldn't remember anything about his private life, except for a faint inkling that there had been an unhappy marriage somewhere. Or was that Sam's other uncle on his mother's side? If James had a friendly, sympathetic wife tucked away, it might make it easier for Bea or Laura to make a full confession. Yet for some reason the thought of James having any kind of wife, sympathetic or otherwise, sent a sharp pain like a toothache lancing through her.

Oh, Laura, you fool, she thought despairingly. You don't even like the man, and that physical magnetism is obviously something he switches on for any woman who comes near him. Didn't Bea say he had a reputation for seducing anything that moved? So you're not really stupid enough to fall for him, are you? Think about Ray instead!

Dutifully she summoned up the image of Ray crouched over a computer screen, patting his thinning fair hair fussily into place and complimenting her on her spreadsheets, but it didn't help. Ray seemed a million miles away, while this disturbing stranger was vibrantly present and impossible to ignore.

A sudden spatter of rain struck the car and she heard the swish of the windscreen wipers starting up. Deliberately she tried to lose herself in the details of the weather—the tug of the wind, the rattle of the raindrops, the hiss of the tyres on the wet road—and she was so successful that soon her pretence of dozing became real. Her eyelids fluttered, she gave a shallow sigh and slept.

She was woken by the movement of the car turning off the tarmac onto a dirt road and lurching up a hill. An involuntary cry of surprise escaped her as she realised where she was. James glanced across and spoke in a polite but distant tone, as if he were talking to a stranger rather than a new member of the family.

'We're nearly there now. Do you want to get out and look at the view?'

He stopped the car and she climbed out and joined him on the crest of the hill. She uttered a low gasp of admiration as she looked at the panorama spread out before them. It had stopped raining and the sea was a deep cobalt blue, which throbbed and heaved around the distant peaks of a group of islands. The sky was filled with the slanting radiance of the late afternoon sun and the breeze from the ocean brought the tang of salt, mingled with the scent of eucalyptus trees and fresh, damp earth.

'That's my house,' said James.

Laura followed the line of his pointing finger and saw a substantial honey-coloured Georgian building tucked into the lee of the hillside so that it was sheltered from the fierce westerly winds. Around it a splash of vivid green colour marked the limits of the garden and beyond that were paddocks full of golden grass where sheep stood in peaceful groups. One or two even had early lambs frisking beside them.

'It's beautiful!' she exclaimed.

'I'm glad you think so,' he replied, with a sardonic lift of his eyebrows. 'I imagine you'll be spending a fair bit of time here if Sam has his way. He loves the land, you know. Even though he has agreed to manage the woollen mill in Hobart for me it's likely that he'll be up here every chance he gets, dealing with the sheep himself. Are you sure you won't get bored?'

There was no mistaking his antagonism now. He doesn't want me to marry his precious nephew one bit, thought Laura indignantly. Or he doesn't want Bea to marry him, which comes to the same thing. He ought to give her...me...a chance!

'I'll manage,' she said coolly. 'I can always dress up in some fancy clothes and put on a fashion parade for the sheep if I get bored, can't I?'

He looked at her sharply, as if he were not sure whether she was joking or not. Then, with a grunt of exasperation, he led the way back to the car. They finished the rest of the journey in silence, but in spite of his unmistakable hostility James couldn't quite overcome his instincts as a host. He carried Laura's bag in from the car, held the door open for her as she entered the house and showed her into a bedroom which was filled with all the comforts a guest could possibly want. Fresh flowers, tissues, a carafe of water and a tin of biscuits, folded towels, a supply of brightly coloured paperbacks. Yet his voice was still curt when he spoke to her.

'I hope you won't mind fending for yourself for a couple of hours. I'm afraid I've still got to go and inspect the prize bull that I intended to look at this morning, but I shouldn't be gone for very long. Just make yourself at home, take a bath, fix a snack—whatever you want to do. I'll cook a proper meal when I get back.'

Left alone, Laura immediately rushed to the telephone to ring Bea, in the hope of having another consultation about her difficult position, but infuriatingly, although the phone rang and rang, Bea didn't answer.

Trying Sam's number didn't help either. All she got there was the answering machine and she left a very terse message on it, instructing Bea to phone her immediately.

After that, she sat down with a groan and ran her hands through her hair. How long was she going to be stranded here? Sometimes in the past airline strikes to Tasmania had gone on for weeks, although in that case the Air Force usually ran an emergency service to get sick people or desperate cases on and off the island. But however desperate Laura might feel, she didn't think the Air Force would consider her a case for emergency evacuation! Well, that just left the overnight boat ferry. If all else failed, perhaps she could hire a car, drive to Devonport and sail back to the mainland.

That still left her with the problem of what was going to happen at the wedding. Even if Bea kept her promise and explained the whole masquerade to James, it still left them with the awkward situation of staging a wedding where the bridegroom's uncle might well murder the bride and the chief bridesmaid. Which Laura couldn't help feeling would cast a damper over the proceedings.

She pinched the bridge of her nose between her thumb and forefinger and shuddered. Why had she ever let Bea talk her into this? Still, there was nothing to be gained by sitting around brooding about it. She might as well accept James's rather grudging invitation and take a look at the place.

It was certainly the kind of house to appeal to her, she decided after a leisurely tour, even if Bea would probably complain that it looked like a museum. All the rooms were graciously proportioned, with carved wooden mantelpieces, lovingly polished antique furniture and dazzling views over the ocean or the hills to the west. Even so, some discreet remodelling had taken place to supply each of the five bedrooms with its own *en suite* bathroom and to provide a kitchen and laundry that had a colonial look but that still concealed the most up-to-date appliances.

Realising she was hungry, Laura opened the refrigerator and found a tempting array of goodies. Smoked salmon, paté, cold meat, a variety of cheeses, vegetables, eggs, a chicken, a bowl of unshelled prawns. She was just about to take out the ingredients for a ham sandwich when a sudden thought struck her. Why not start cooking dinner herself?

With James's disturbing presence temporarily removed, her antagonism was beginning to ebb away and she felt more like her usual self. Calm, sensible, anxious to smooth things over. Even that long, sultry, assessing look he had given her when they first met seemed more and more a product of her own fevered imagination. Probably the truth was that he was simply a conscientious uncle, worried that Sam and Bea were embarking on marriage too soon. And if that was the case, it was up to her to try and placate him.

She must do all that she could to show him that she and Bea were both mature, reliable people. And what better way than by pampering him a bit? He would be tired when he came in from inspecting the bull and it was hardly likely that he would really want to make a meal. Of course, he might feel that she was intruding, but on the other hand he had invited her to help herself to a snack. And perhaps it would even soften him up for the moment when they made their final confession. Humming to herself, she lifted out the dish of prawns...

* * *

'That was an excellent meal,' admitted James as he drained the last of his coffee with a sigh of satisfaction.

Laura looked at the table with a touch of complacency. Avocado filled with prawns in a seafood dressing had been followed by a stuffed roast chicken with Greek baked potatoes, zucchini and tomatoes and an apple crumble with cinnamon topping and whipped cream. James had opened a bottle of Houghton's white burgundy and they had brewed fresh coffee to complete the meal. The conversation had gone well too, and she had seen the surprised flash of respect in his eyes when she had made a casual remark about government agricultural policy.

Although they were still fencing with each other, she thought she detected a softening in his initial antagonism towards her. And, rather reluctantly, she had to admit that she found him very interesting company.

'Would you like some more coffee?' she asked.

'All right,' he agreed, rising to his feet. 'Why don't you bring it into the living room? I'm going to set a match to the fire in there.'

As he spoke a sudden, sharp gust of wind set the windowpanes rattling, and a spatter of drops struck against the glass. Striding across the room, James closed the cedar shutters firmly, shutting out the gathering darkness and rain. It was a simple action and yet it made Laura feel odd—as if they were holing up together in some snug, little lair and turning their backs on the outside world. There was something alarming about the idea of drawing close to a hissing, crackling orange fire with James Fraser while a storm raged and buffeted outside.

Suddenly she became aware that he was watching her through narrowed eyes and she dropped her gaze self-consciously. Her heart raced and she no longer felt so certain that she had imagined that sensual glance he had given her earlier in the day. What if he really was wondering what it would be like to take off her clothes and lay her down on the sheepskin rug in the firelight? Bea had once told her that she had a very expressive face, but she hoped devoutly that that wasn't true! If her face was expressing half the things she was thinking tonight, she was in big trouble . . .

'I'll get the coffee,' she said, retreating into the kitchen.

When she came into the living room ten minutes later, James was crouched on the hearth, feeding the flames with more substantial lengths of wood. The glow from the firelight made his eyes glitter and highlighted the rugged contours of his face, making him look like some primitive caveman. Suddenly he looked up at her with an expression that made Laura's breath catch in her throat.

No, she hadn't imagined that silent, sensual appraisal earlier in the day, for he was doing it again now. And this time she was powerless even to turn her head away. All she could do was stare at him with her lips half parted and her shoulders tensed as if to ward off danger.

Before he went out to inspect the bull, he had changed into denim jeans and an open-necked flannel shirt which was now rolled up to his elbows, revealing muscular forearms spiked with dark hair that glowed bronze in the firelight. As he rose to his feet, still trapping her in that mesmerising gaze, she felt again that she was a waif, a stray, an outcast seeking shelter in a hostile world. And it didn't seem at all likely that this threatening stranger was going to take pity on her.

The cup clattered in its saucer as she handed it to him.

He added sugar, stirred the coffee and drank it down without ever taking his eyes off her. Then he reached behind him and set the empty china on the mantelpiece.

'Tell me something,' he said harshly. 'What's the real truth behind all this?'

CHAPTER TWO

LAURA'S stomach gave a sickening lurch and she stared at him in alarm, momentarily diverted from her unwelcome attraction to him. Obviously he had guessed that she wasn't Bea and now he wanted an explanation. Well, the only thing she could do was to give him one, apologise abjectly and leave as soon as possible. She only hoped that he wouldn't take his anger out on her sister once he learnt what they had done.

'Look, I can see you've realised that something is seriously wrong,' she began awkwardly. 'You must feel that I'm here under false pretences, but I—'

'I wouldn't go that far,' he cut in. 'After all, Sam is legally an adult and he has a perfect right to marry you. I also know from his telephone conversations that he's head over heels in love with you. What worries me is what you're hoping to get out of it, Bea.'

Bea. So he hadn't guessed at all. Laura's wildly beating heart slowly subsided to its normal rhythm, although she still felt shaken. She stared at James in dismay, feeling as if her brain had turned to cotton wool. What on earth was she supposed to say now?

'There's no need to look at me as if I'm an executioner!' he continued impatiently. 'It's just that if you're marrying Sam, I want to know more about you. And for heaven's sake tell me the truth!'

'What do you mean?' blurted out Laura.

'I mean, what do you want out of life? What motivates you? What's your greatest need?'

26

Something in the urgency of his voice mesmerised her, so that she was unable to lie. A wry smile twisted her lips as she gazed into the dark tunnel of her past. Memories came crowding back to her—of the first frozen grief after her mother's death, her dogged determination to look after Bea and not be parted from her, her decision that she would work hard and be responsible and make a future for them both. She gave a faint, mirthless whisper of laughter.

'Security,' she said.

She saw a brief flash of hostility in James's eyes, but he nodded his head.

'Well, that's honest at all events,' he retorted. 'And marrying is certainly one way of getting it. But these days most girls train for a career as well, just in case Mr Wonderful doesn't show up. Were you so certain of your charms that you didn't feel the need to train for anything?'

Laura flinched.

'I did!' she exclaimed hotly. 'I—'

She broke off, remembering too late that she was supposed to be Bea.

'You did what, exactly?'

'I studied horticulture for a while.'

'So you have a diploma?' he demanded.

'No.'

'Why not?'

'I dropped out,' she said, with a defiant lift of her chin.

'I see. And what did you do then? Start looking round immediately for a rich husband?'

'No!' flared Laura, distractedly trying to remember exactly what Bea had done. There had been a period on the dole, a brief job as a croupier in a casino and a year on a working holiday, where the work had been mostly making beds in motels or waitressing in crummy cafés. Hastily she decided not to mention any of that. 'I got a job in a dress shop and then they asked me to do some catwalk modelling and suddenly my career took off. It was just luck, really.'

'You rely a lot on luck, don't you?' said James in a hard voice. 'As far as I can see, it was also just luck that Sam fell in love with you. Are you going to depend on luck to make your marriage work too?'

His sarcasm was so burning that Laura felt shrivelled by it. For several moments she looked at him in dismay, unable to find any sensible answer. At last she dropped her gaze, unable to offer any adequate defence.

'Why do you hate me so much?' she whispered.

'I don't hate you,' he snapped. 'I simply think that you're young and naïve and capable of doing a great deal of harm. What's more, I'd like to make you think before it's too late. You're...how old? Twenty-three? And Sam's twenty-four! Well, to me you seem very young, and from all I've heard about you you're also very immature. I simply don't think it's a good idea for you to rush into marriage. In my opinion you should wait until you're older and until you've known each other longer. You don't have the experience to see the pitfalls of what you're doing, but I do.'

'What pitfalls?' demanded Laura.

To her dismay he stepped forward and seized her by the shoulders. The room seemed to spin around her and for one wild moment she stood motionless, trapped by the hypnotic golden intensity of his gaze. A shameful rush of desire surged through her at his touch, so hot and raw and primitive that she was shocked by it. Try as she might, she could not shut out her unbearable awareness of his masculinity, of the heat and power and size of him as he loomed above her. His fingers bit into her flesh, making her feel soft and boneless. She took a shallow, fluttering breath and fought down an insane urge to wind her arms around his neck and lift her parted lips to his.

Darting him a panicky glance from under half closed eyelids, she saw that he was fully aware of her response to him. Not only that, but he clearly revelled in it. The amusement that curled his lips sent a hot flush of embarrassment flooding into her cheeks. Why was he doing this? Did he feel an equal measure of desire for her? Or was he simply trying to make a fool of her?

'Let's start with the pitfalls of attraction to another man,' he murmured tauntingly. 'You're so young and impressionable. What will you do, Bea, when you find yourself uncontrollably attracted to somebody else, as I'm sure you will?'

The way he had drawled the words 'somebody else' left her in no doubt of his meaning. That hoarse, smoky baritone was so blatantly suggestive that she could have slapped his face. How could he humiliate her like this, especially when he thought she was about to marry Sam? And why did he have to degrade her so pitilessly by gloating over her reaction to him? Didn't he have any compassion at all? And how could she still feel this treacherous yearning for him, when she resented him so much?

Suddenly Laura lost her temper, and her anger with herself was transformed into fury with James. Breaking free of his hold, she stepped back a pace and glared at him.

'You pompous brute!' she shouted and then paused, struggling incoherently for speech. She couldn't tell him the truth—that she despised him for his prejudice towards Bea and for the insulting way he was playing sexual games with her. But she could, and would, tell him what she thought of his own attitudes and values! Who was he to lay down the law to her when his own love life was nothing to be proud of?

She took a deep breath and her words came out in an angry torrent. 'I may be young, but I'm not stupid. And where has your precious wisdom and experience got you? Just tell me that! You must be at least thirty-five years old, but you're not happily married, are you? So what use was all your caution to you? If you ask me, the best thing you can do in relationships is to trust your instincts, close your eyes and jump! All right, you might get hurt, you might even hurt somebody else. But at least you'll be alive and feeling and breathing and knowing what it means to be in love, not just playing it safe. In my opinion, you're the one who's naïve if you think you can get a guarantee of happiness just by refusing to take any risks!'

Her own vehemence astonished her, and she tried to tell herself that she was only expressing Bea's philosophy of life, but that didn't seem to explain why her outburst had left her so agitated. She saw that James was staring at her with mild amazement and she folded her arms around her body and took deep, calming breaths. Too late, she realised how heated she had been and a pang of guilt went through her.

'I'm sorry, I shouldn't have said all that,' she muttered. 'I'm a guest in your house and it was very rude. Please forgive me.'

He shrugged, as if her outburst hadn't troubled him in the least. Her stinging attack on his own way of life seemed to have left him completely unmoved. The faint, flickering smile on his lips didn't waver for an instant as he returned her gaze. Then he spoke in a measured tone, as if he were thinking aloud.

'There's just one thing that puzzles me about you, Beatrice. You virtually admitted to me earlier that you weren't in love with Sam and that you were only concerned with security, and yet you've just treated me to a passionate outburst in favour of falling in love and taking risks in relationships. Isn't that rather a contradiction? Can you explain it to me?'

Laura's mouth opened and closed as if she were a stranded goldfish. Yes, it was a contradiction, although she probably could explain it if she simply told the truth. All she had to say was a few, simple sentences. Bea is in love with Sam, but I'm not. I care about security, but she doesn't. She believes in taking risks, but I don't. When I was shouting so passionately about love, I was simply being her mouthpiece, saying what she'd say if she were here. Or was I? Is it possible that I really believe all that stuff about risk-taking myself deep down? She stared at James with a stricken expression, appalled by this moment of self-discovery.

'The truth is that there are times when I don't even know what I want myself,' she muttered, dropping her eyes. 'Times when I don't even know who I really am.'

She found that he was towering over her again and that his hand was lifting her chin, forcing her to look at him, forcing her to see the strange, fierce expression in his tawny eyes. His thumb touched her cheekbone, caressing the skin in a slow whorl as he looked down at her.

'Then I think you ought to find out before you get married next week,' he said hoarsely. 'Don't you?'

Every nerve in her body seemed to jangle as she felt anew that hot, unwelcome thrill of physical attraction towards him. It would be easy, fatally easy to let herself sway forward against him and find herself caught in his crushing embrace. The silence between them lengthened and she felt almost certain that James was experiencing the same aching, primitive sense of need that was disturbing her so profoundly. But she felt equally certain that this was nothing but a game to him. Angrily she jerked herself free of his touch.

'Look, what's it got to do with you?' she demanded.

He caught her by the wrist, swinging her back to face him.

'Plenty,' he snapped. 'I like Sam a lot and I don't want him being made unhappy by some twitty little girl in ridiculous clothes who doesn't even know what she wants.'

'Ridiculous clothes?' echoed Laura incredulously, glancing down at Bea's long striped cardigan. 'Oh, so that's what this is about, is it? It's just blind, simple prejudice. You disapprove of me because I'm a model, don't you?'

'That's ridiculous! If I disapprove of you, it's because I suspect you're unstable and likely to skip out of this marriage at the first sign of difficulty.'

All Laura's old insecurities came rushing back and she felt the blood surge into her cheeks in a burning rush.

'You're only saying that because of the background I come from!' she shouted accusingly. 'Just because I grew up in foster homes, you don't think I can sustain a stable marriage.'

'That's utter rubbish! I wasn't even thinking about that!'

'You were!' cried Laura, her voice rising and growing more rapid. 'I know you were! You think I'm not good enough for Sam, don't you? Your family is rich and respectable and important and nobody ever gets divorced in it, so you don't think I'm good enough to be allowed in the door, do you?'

James glared at her.

'I didn't say that!' he retorted in exasperation. 'Anyway, who said my family never got divorced? Sam's father Adrian is divorced, I'm divorced, and the only reason my sister Wendy isn't divorced is because she never bothered to marry any of her lovers.'

Laura felt an odd prickling sensation that was a mixture of pain and relief at the news that James was divorced. For some ridiculous reason it hurt her to know that he had ever been married, and yet she couldn't help feeling absurdly glad that the marriage was definitely over. And then she saw the grim twist to his lips, the harsh etching of the lines around his mouth—was it over for him?

'*Are* you divorced? Why?'

'That's none of your damned business! It's irrelevant anyway, and I don't know why I even mentioned it. It happened years ago and I'll never be fool enough to get married again. I was simply making the point that—'

'Oh, I see!' she interrupted. 'You're disillusioned with marriage, so you have to try and turn everyone else off it too. What right do you have to tell me that I'm frivolous and selfish and that I'll skip out at the first sign of difficulty? You know nothing about me!'

His face darkened.

'I know you're planning to marry Sam for financial security and I know there's a hell of a lot more to marriage than that. If you think a big house in Sandy Bay is going to make you happy, little girl, you've got a lot of growing up to do!'

'Don't you "little girl" me!' shouted Laura. 'If you think that because you've bought us a house you can be the power broker in our marriage, well, you can forget it! We don't need your house and we won't take it. I'll tell Sam to refuse it. We'll buy our own damned house.'

'Oh, don't be ridiculous! It's nothing to do with my trying to be a "power broker" in your marriage, as you put it. You've got a perfect right to own that house, you and Sam.'

Laura was momentarily sidetracked. As an accountant she sensed an interesting complication. When she spoke again, her voice was quieter.

'What do you mean? You're the one paying for it, aren't you?'

'Yes,' growled James. 'But only because of the way my father's will was left. You see, Sam's father has never had any sense handling money, it runs through his fingers like water, so my father left his share of the estate to me, as well as my own. He knew if my brother Adrian got hold of it he'd squander it before his kids ever saw it.'

'Whereas you—' prompted Laura.

James heaved an exasperated sigh and ran his fingers through his black hair so that it stood up in wild disorder.

'Whereas I'm the sensible, responsible one,' he said bitterly. 'The one that pays off mortgages and tends the stock and budgets for the taxes and gets the rest of the family out of trouble when they blunder into it. Somebody has to be reliable or they would all come adrift. My father knew I'd take care of Sam and the others, so he left everything in my hands.'

That sounds just like me, thought Laura with an unwilling twinge of sympathy. She remembered how earnestly she had argued with the welfare worker when she was twenty-one to convince her that she could provide a home for Bea on her salary as a first-year accountant. And how much she had sacrificed to keep her promise to her dying mother that she would take care of her sister. All those lost opportunities for dates and parties and good times flashed before her eyes, but she felt not so much virtuous as utterly fed up. If James had gone through the same thing with his family, she pitied him! Even if he was a callous, manipulative womaniser, nobody deserved to be Mr Fixit all the time.

'Don't you ever get sick of being the sensible one?' she burst out.

'Yes,' said James grimly.

'What would you have liked to do if you hadn't had to be the person that everybody else relied on?' she asked curiously.

His eyes narrowed and he seemed to be looking at something far away.

'I would have gone up to the Great Barrier Reef for at least a year and been a beachcomber,' he replied without hesitation. 'It would have been great to go surfing or riding horses along those long white beaches and lie around under the palm trees for a year or so. Mind you, I probably would have got sick of it after that. I suspect I'm the hard-working, ambitious type deep down. Still, it would have been fun.'

'It's not very different from what I would have done,' murmured Laura half to herself. 'I would have loved to go off to Queensland and spend months hiking through the rainforests and collecting wildflowers without ever having to worry about going to work and being responsible.'

James cast her a frowning, baffled look.

'Then why didn't you just do it?' he asked. 'You studied horticulture, didn't you, at least for a while? And from what you've told me, it doesn't sound as if there was any strongly developed work ethic standing in your way.'

Laura felt as if a chill had invaded the room. Why did she keep forgetting who she was supposed to be? Of course, James was right. If her sister had wanted to travel around and hike through rainforests, she would simply have done it. Whereas good, old, boring, sensible Laura wouldn't dream of doing anything so rash. Just as she wouldn't dream of flinging aside caution and plunging headlong into a torrid affair with James.

A sudden blaze of rebellion ignited inside her. If only I thought it was me personally that he wanted, instead of any woman who comes near him! she thought despairingly. Or if only Bea and I hadn't deceived him like this and he didn't think I was a scheming gold-digger! I wish, I wish... Then she caught the implacable glint of hostility in his tawny eyes and she heaved a faint, defeated sigh. What was the point of wishing? It was all useless. The best thing she could do was to avoid him as much as possible and pray for a miracle to get her out of this mess.

'Well, we're very different people, aren't we?' she said coolly. 'I don't suppose I can expect you to understand anything I do. If you'll excuse me, I think I'll go to bed now.'

As she moved towards the door he put out his hand to stop her. To her surprise, the antagonism in his voice was suddenly softened by something else. A glimmer of respect, perhaps? Or even a wary friendliness. Laura had the impression that he was struggling to be fair.

'Listen,' he muttered. 'I'm not necessarily opposed to you, Beatrice. You've obviously got a lot more character and intelligence than I was led to expect. But there are two things in life I hate. One is deceit, the other is disloyalty. At least you seem to be honest and genuine, but I can't help worrying about whether you'll be loyal to Sam in the long run. So I'm warning you, think again about whether you want to go through with this marriage.'

Laura woke the next morning with a feeling of intense misgiving, mingled with a ridiculous fluttery sense of excitement. As she showered and dressed she tried to focus her thoughts. There was no doubt that she had landed herself in serious trouble. In one way she was tempted to phone for a hire car and flee northwards to the ferry, but a few moments' reflection convinced her that she couldn't leave without an explanation.

James still believed that she was Bea and he would be expecting her to stay, so it would be the height of rudeness to vanish without telling him why. He might be opposed to Bea's forthcoming marriage, but he didn't deserve anything as dreadful as that! Besides, there were practical difficulties—he might call the police and put out a missing person's report on her if she simply left without a word. Yet she shrank from trying to explain their idiotic masquerade to him. Let Bea do that when she arrived!

The trouble was that with every extra minute she spent in his company, she felt as if she were sinking deeper and deeper into quicksand. Even though they had quarrelled last night, she still couldn't deny the treacherous attraction she felt towards him. But there could be no future for them. Not when she suspected him of trying to seduce her simply for entertainment. And not when he found out about all the lies she had told him...

Well, he would have to know before the wedding, and her stomach contracted in morbid dread at the thought of the scene that would ensue when he did find out. Had she really been crazy enough to think that it would be quite exciting to have James shouting and storming at her? The truth was likely to be utterly different! She could just picture the cold look of contempt that would come over his face when he discovered how she and Bea had tricked him.

Would he refuse to take part in the wedding? At the moment he was supposed to be giving Bea away, since she didn't have a father to do it, but who could blame him if he refused to take part? He didn't seem like the kind of man who would grin and shrug his shoulders if somebody made a fool of him. Laura suspected that a formidable temper smouldered beneath his urbane exterior. He wasn't in the least bit long-suffering, like Raymond.

Raymond! Oh, heavens, she had forgotten all about Raymond... She'd been supposed to give him an answer to his proposal yesterday, so what on earth would he think of her? She had never failed to keep a promise before! Even as the thought crossed her mind she knew what her answer was going to be and knew that it didn't matter that she had broken her promise. After the whirlwind emotions which James had roused in her during the last twenty-four hours, there was no possible way that she could marry Raymond. All the same, he deserved an answer.

Feeling as if she were ringing up the dentist to make an appointment for a wisdom tooth extraction, Laura picked up the phone.

'Ray?'

'Laura! I was halfway through shaving! What on earth happened? I thought you were supposed to get in touch with me yesterday. You didn't show up to work and your secretary said you'd taken a day's leave without any real explanation.'

His tone was faintly querulous and Laura felt a niggling sense of exasperation, followed by an urge to get the ordeal over.

'Yes, I'm sorry,' she said shortly. 'There was a sudden hitch to do with Bea's wedding and I had to fly down to Tasmania unexpectedly. Now that I'm here I'll be staying for a few days, but never mind that. What I really rang to tell you is that ... I can't marry you.'

'That's a bit abrupt,' protested Ray mildly. She thought she heard a faint scraping sound in the background. Was he continuing to shave while he talked? 'Can't you give me some reasons?'

'There's only one reason, Ray. I don't love you.'

He laughed indulgently, the same sort of laugh she had heard once when she had told him the petty cash tin was short of fifteen cents, although even then he had kept going through the books relentlessly until he found the error.

'Love!' he snorted. 'We're both mature adults, Laura. Do we need to make such a fuss about terminology?'

Laura felt a pang of irrational antagonism so fierce that if Ray had been in the room, she would have picked up the phone and thrown it at him. Terminology, indeed! And if you got rid of love, what did you do? Spend the rest of your life having dry little conversations about a few missing cents in the petty cash tin? No, thanks! There had to be more to the universe than that!

'Well, I do,' she said. 'I'm sorry, Ray, but I guess that's the end of it.'

'Laura, are you sick or something? You don't sound at all like yourself. Look, don't rush into a decision. Wait until Beatrice's wedding is over and talk to me about it then. By the way, did I tell you I got the Simmons and Waterman contract? Quite a coup, really.'

'Good for you,' retorted Laura coldly, and hung up.

As she moved away from the phone it occurred to her that the whole conversation had resembled a business discussion about some minor appointment which could be cancelled without too much difficulty. The realisation made her feel surer than ever that she was doing the right thing. After all, a decision to get married was a pretty important event, and ought to be accompanied by some very powerful feelings. Even if a proposal was refused, she felt that it ought to be more than just a passing disturbance in somebody's day. Raymond hadn't sounded upset, merely aggrieved. And, if she was going to be honest, her own reaction was mainly one of relief, which was crazy. If she had just refused a proposal of marriage from James Fraser, she was certain that she would have felt shaken to the core by the experience.

'But if James proposed to me,' she said aloud, 'maybe I wouldn't refuse anyway.'

She stopped suddenly in her tracks with a jolt of dismay as she realised what she had just said. A low groan escaped her.

Oh, Lord, she really had it badly, didn't she? What did James have to do with anything? It was hardly likely that he was ever going to ask her to marry him. As a matter of fact, his main preoccupation at the moment seemed to be trying to talk her out of getting married, but was that really just because he thought that she...or Bea...was too young? Or could it possibly be that he was genuinely attracted to her himself and not merely playing games with her?

Shaking her head, she dismissed the thought as being too silly for words and began to get dressed. Not that she had many clothes to choose from. Believing that she would only be staying in Tasmania for one day, she hadn't bothered to bring much with her, and only her habitual caution had made her pack any clothes at all. What she had brought was definitely in her style rather than Bea's. A long viyella nightdress, plain underwear and sensible shoes, a dark blue knit suit with a little gold brooch to pin on the jacket and a severely cut black coat which she had bought in Florence on her holidays two years ago.

That should baffle James after the violently coloured long cardigan she had worn yesterday! And perhaps seeing her with her hair in a chignon would shake his smug notions about how young and irresponsible she was. An impish sense of mischief began to mingle with her guilt.

As she'd expected, James gave her a startled glance when she walked into the kitchen. He was standing at the stove, stirring something in a frying pan, and the appetising smell of bacon and tomatoes wafted across to meet her.

'That was good timing,' he announced, tilting the frying pan and dividing the food evenly onto two plates. Switching off the stove, he handed one of the plates to Laura and gestured at a table by the window which was already set with a checked red and white cloth, orange juice, butter, jam and all the other paraphernalia of breakfast. Laura gave him a worldly wise smile as he poured some juice for her and passed her the toast.

'You look very nice,' he said with approval, glancing at her dark suit. 'That's an extremely suitable outfit for seeing the vicar about the wedding.'

Laura choked on a mouthful of bacon.

'What did you say?' she gulped.

James leaned back in his chair and his eyes narrowed. There was an almost wolfish quality to his expression which made Laura's blood run cold.

'I said that's a very suitable outfit for visiting the vicar about the wedding,' he repeated, with a mildness that was almost sinister. 'Didn't I tell you that he phoned me yesterday and suggested that we should have a proper rehearsal for the ceremony? Unless you've changed your mind about whether there's going to be a wedding?'

She stared at him with the stricken horror of a baby rabbit which had just noticed the swooping shadow of a hawk. Playing this masquerade to one person was bad enough, but if she was now going to be forced to convince the vicar that she was Bea, she would simply crack up.

Several courses of action occurred to her, all of them equally ridiculous. She could hide under the table and never come out, she could hitch-hike to the end of the island and then swim, or she could agree with James that the wedding ought to be cancelled. The last one was the solution that had most appeal, except that the choice was utterly farcical. She wasn't the one getting married anyway.

'You're not really going to go ahead with this, are you?' demanded James.

His voice was harsh, and to her astonishment his right hand suddenly shot out, seizing her wrist with such force that she cried out. His grip softened marginally, but he continued to gaze at her with an intensity that almost scorched her. She found that her heart was hammering with a wild exultation. He is attracted to me! she thought dizzily. It's the same for him as it is for me. Then the absurdity of her situation struck her again and she shuddered.

'There's nothing I can do to stop this wedding now,' she said jerkily, dropping her eyes and avoiding his gaze.

'That's rubbish! You're just letting social pressure and embarrassment force you into it, Bea, because you can't face the humiliation of crying off at the last moment. But you know you're doing something very wrong, don't you?'

'You know you're doing something very wrong, don't you?' The words seared her as if he had scorched them into her conscience with a branding iron, but of course James wasn't aware of their double meaning.

'Please let me go!' she blurted out, wrenching away from him.

'All right,' he snapped, releasing her. 'But don't say I didn't warn you. If you go ahead and marry Sam without really loving him and being sure that you're ready for lifelong commitment, you're going to regret it, and I'm sure the vicar will tell you the same thing. Why don't you discuss it with him when you see him today?'

So he was back on that, was he? Laura stared at him in alarm.

'What do you mean—when I see him today?'

'I told you—he rang up and suggested a rehearsal. Some of the music is rather tricky and the organist wants to run through it. I've explained that Sam is still stranded on the mainland, but the vicar is very anxious for us to go ahead with it anyway. He likes to have all the details right and we've got you here as the bride, which is the most important thing.'

Laura felt as if she were trapped in the middle of a nightmare. Go through the wedding rehearsal and pretend she was the bride? This was getting worse and worse! Wishing the floor would open and swallow her up, she tried a desperate, last-minute tactic.

'Oh, I don't think we should have the rehearsal without the bridegroom! Can't we just cancel it?'

'No, we can't,' growled James, and the pupils of his eyes seemed to narrow into pitiless slits. 'I'll stand in for Sam as your husband. Maybe it will jolt you into thinking about the significance of what you're doing.'

The church was a quaint little sandstone building standing on a gentle green hill overlooking the sea. On the noticeboard at the gate a rather faded sign bore the text 'FEED MY LAMBS, FEED MY SHEEP', which seemed particularly appropriate, since a couple of merino ewes had escaped from a nearby paddock and were nibbling the grass that grew in lush clumps around the weathered gravestones.

If she had not been so agitated, Laura would have been enchanted by the pink frothy blossom which covered the cherry trees in the rectory garden next door and by the drifts of daffodils that tossed their heads beneath the bare oak trees. As it was, she felt as if she were being led off to execution as James put his arm around her shoulders and escorted her relentlessly up the path to the rectory door. A chubby, balding man with pink cheeks and thick horn-rimmed spectacles answered their second ring and beamed at them.

'James, good to see you! And this is the bride, is it? Nice to meet you at last, Beatrice. My name's Bill Archer.

I've known young Sam since he was pinching the apples from the trees in my orchard during his school holidays, and it couldn't give me greater pleasure than to be officiating at his wedding. I gather he couldn't be with us today, though?'

'No,' said Laura in a wan voice. 'There's an airline strike.'

'It's all right, though,' added James in velvety tones. 'I've offered to stand in instead. I think Beatrice ought to have this final chance for quiet contemplation about the meaning of holy matrimony.'

The vicar looked taken aback.

'Er, well, yes,' he agreed, tugging at his earlobe. 'And to get the hymns right and that sort of thing too. Christine, my dear! We're just going over to the church to run through young Sam's wedding service. Why don't you come with us?'

Laura had thought the agony couldn't get any worse, but once she found herself inside the church she realised she'd been wrong. The building itself was beautiful, with its stained glass windows sparkling in the sun, its gleaming wooden pews smelling of lemon furniture polish and the fresh flowers that decked the altar. If she'd been going to be married, she couldn't think of a nicer place to do it than this. But within the next five minutes she began to feel as if she were in a torture chamber as the other participants in the rehearsal gradually assembled. While the vicar made the necessary introductions she looked around her as despairingly as if she were a hostage in the clutches of a gang of terrorists.

'All right, Bea, you've met my wife Christine and myself. Now, the lady in the green is Audrey Phillips, our organist, and behind her is John Timmins, who is going to be the best man. That leaves Peter Clark, my sexton, who won't be taking part in the actual ceremony but has very kindly offered to give you away just for today, since James, who is going to have that privilege at the real wedding, is otherwise occupied at the moment. Now, have we forgotten anyone? Oh, dear, that's awkward! We don't have a bridesmaid, do we? What a pity your sister Laura couldn't be here!'

'Yes, isn't it?' agreed Laura faintly.

'Oh, I'll take her place,' offered the vicar's wife. 'Now, let's get started. Go and stand on the chancel steps, Bill, and tell them what you want them to do.'

'It's not too difficult. Once Audrey strikes up the "Wedding March", you take Peter's arm, Bea. Make a slow procession down the centre aisle, so everyone can have a good look at you, and when you arrive here the bridegroom will step forward to meet you. You both face me and the father—that's Peter—will move a little to the left and the best man to the right. You hand your flowers to the bridesmaid and we go ahead with the ceremony. Has everyone got that?'

Suppressing a wild urge to run outside and hide behind a convenient gravestone, Laura trudged to the back of the church and linked arms with the sexton. As they glided down the aisle together she tried to imagine the upturned smiling faces of family and friends, but all she could think of was her own embarrassment and guilt. Until the moment when Peter Clark deftly stepped away from her and James moved forward to meet her. In that instant she felt as if the entire church, with its sunbeams and joyful music and well-meaning onlookers, had vanished into a void, leaving her alone with a man who had every reason to disapprove of her.

And yet disapproval didn't seem to be the only emotion that was burning inside James Fraser. As he looked down at her with his tawny eyes narrowed she caught a glimpse of something that made her feel totally breathless. Some raw, urgent, primal need, as if he had vowed to conquer her and make her his own. A faint tremor went through her limbs and she felt her breast heave agonisingly.

Bill Archer's voice began to drone in the background, but after a while the words penetrated Laura's reverie and made her wince with renewed shame. When he took her hand and put it into James's, she realised that it felt as cold as a slab of ice. James seemed to notice it too, for he frowned thoughtfully at her as he took the ring from the best man and slipped it onto her finger. But the worst moment of all came when he recited his vows. Or rather Sam's.

'With this ring I thee wed, with my body I thee worship, and with all my worldly goods I thee endow.'

Laura flinched as she realised what a mockery she was making of a sacred ceremony. And, quite apart from the misery she felt about that, she could not suppress an irrational surge of longing to know what it would be like to be James's bride in reality. How would she feel if he knew who she really was and genuinely wanted to marry her? How would she feel if this powerful, disturbing man was gazing down at her so searingly and she knew that Bill Archer was really on the point of pronouncing them man and wife? How would she feel if she knew that soon they were going to go away on a honeymoon which would mark the start of their life together? Catching her breath, she made her way back up the aisle with James at her side.

Afterwards Christine Archer treated them all to excellent coffee and date scones in her living room, but

Laura had lost her appetite. The vicar looked at her with concern.

'You're very pale, Bea. Are you feeling all right?'

'It's just bride's collywobbles!' insisted Christine. 'I know how you feel, my dear. I felt exactly the same at my wedding rehearsal.'

'Oh. Did you?' said Laura doubtfully.

'Of course, if there's anything really troubling you about the wedding,' put in James, 'you really ought to have a talk to Bill about it immediately.'

Laura dropped her teaspoon with a resounding clatter.

'I don't think that will be necessary,' she babbled.

Afterwards James bundled her into the car in disapproving silence and continued to scowl as they drove along the coast road. However, he did not take the turn-off to the farm, but instead chose a dirt road which led down to a secluded beach. In a clearing among the sand hills, he stopped the car.

'What are we doing?' asked Laura in a bewildered voice.

'I need to think and I think best when I'm walking along beaches. Get out.'

His tone was curt, almost rude. Feeling even more uneasy than she had been in the church, Laura obeyed. Without a backward glance at her, he strode along a boardwalk track that led between the silvery sand hills with their rippling mantle of grey marram grass. Out on the beach the full force of the wind hit them, snatching away her breath, but the experience was exhilarating.

The sea was a bright, sparkling blue, with long, driving breakers of white foam that crashed on the sand, and overhead the sky was a paler blue, with a few puffs of white cloud. Seagulls wheeled and shrieked, scanning the water for food, but otherwise the only sound was the crash of the waves and the occasional mournful bleating of a sheep from a nearby headland.

Lowering his head, as if he were planning a particularly vicious rugby tackle, James thrust his hands into the pockets of his brown corduroy trousers and strode off along the beach, apparently indifferent to whether she followed him or not. For a moment she was tempted simply to go back to the car and wait, but some contrary impulse sent her toiling along in his wake, although she almost had to run to keep up with him. Sand got into her shoes, the wind blew her neat chignon into untidy tendrils of hair around her face and once or twice she gave a little shriek and jumped out of the way as an onrushing wave came too far.

'What's the matter?' she shouted above the thunder of the wind and waves.

Stupid question. Everything in the world was the matter and it was all her fault. Hers and Bea's. And there was nothing obvious she could do to set things right now, although she was appalled by the trouble she had caused. To her surprise, James suddenly seized her hand and dragged her up the powdery white beach to the crest of the sand hills and down into a hollow beyond. Suddenly the clamour of the wind was silenced, as if by magic, and she found that she could hear subtler sounds. The uneven rasp of James's breathing, the thudding of her own heart.

To her alarm, he cupped her face in his hands.

'You're not really going ahead with this farcical marriage, are you?' he demanded.

She jerked her head away as if he had slapped her.

'Please! Stop it!' she cried in a low, tormented voice. 'I don't want to talk about it.'

'You'll ruin your own life and Sam's too,' he said savagely. 'You can't possibly marry him.'

'Why can't I?'

'Because you really want to go to bed with me.'

She gasped and looked up at him with wildly dilated eyes.

'That's not true.'

'Isn't it? Tell me, Beatrice, what's it like when Sam kisses you?'

Beatrice. Laura dropped her gaze and turned crimson.

'That's none of your business.'

But he seemed determined to make it his business. With an impatient oath, he tore off the band which held her hair confined and let it tumble in riotous profusion around her shoulders. Then, threading his fingers through the disordered strands, he forced her head back so that she had to look at him. His face was so close to hers that she could catch the spicy whiff of his aftershave and see the dark shadow of his beard beneath his skin. An alarming weakness overtook her as she wondered how it would feel to reach up her fingers and stroke the rugged outline of his jaw.

'When he kisses you, does it make your heart pound as if you're running a marathon?' he demanded. 'Do you feel as if you'd die if you lost him? Does a crowded room go still and strange and silent for you when he comes into it? Do you feel a need more urgent than anything you've ever imagined for him? Do you love him, Bea?'

All the bizarre events of the last forty-eight hours crowded in upon her. What a mess it was—herself and Raymond, Bea and Sam, James, the wedding rehearsal ... So many tangles, all starting from one insignificant little lie like a dropped stitch in a pattern. Tell him the truth! her conscience urged. Tell him now! She opened her mouth to speak, then looked at his intent, brooding face and her nerve failed her. Twice she moistened her lips, looking at him with a wordless longing to confess and be forgiven, then she dropped her head, avoiding his gaze.

'Yes,' she whispered. 'I do.'

'Liar,' he breathed, and hauled her into his arms. 'This is what a kiss should be like.'

Her stomach dived at the realisation of what he was about to do, and then he was doing it and nothing else mattered. Laura had been kissed before, but never like this. She willed herself not to respond, but it was useless. James's muscles were as hard as whipcords as he trapped her between his thighs and forced her backwards. His powerful hands were splayed against her shoulderblades so that she was in no real danger of falling and yet an extraordinary dizziness rushed through her. A dizziness that only increased when she saw the flare of longing in his eyes, the hungry need in his parted lips, the tension that contorted his features. Then his warm, demanding mouth covered hers and she forgot everything in a hot, engulfing surge of unfamiliar excitement.

Ruthlessly his tongue thrust to meet hers, and the intimate contact unleashed a tingling current of sensation deep inside her. Every part of her seemed to be throbbing and aching with yearning for a deeper union. His grip tightened around her and she felt the hard, urgent heat of his arousal pressed against her. She should have been shocked and outraged. Instead a heady sense of exultation surged through her and suddenly she felt as violently out of control as if she had just catapulted over the edge of a steep, thundering waterfall. Her ears roared, her eyelids fluttered shut and she swayed against him, glorying in the unfamiliar tingling sensations that were pulsating through her.

James uttered a low groan as she arched backwards, pressing her breasts against him, and his kisses grew even more passionate. His mouth plundered hers in a series of assaults that half alarmed and half enthralled her. But she did not resist. Instead, she wound her arms around his neck, lifted her lips to his and kissed him back as wantonly as if nothing existed except the roaring sea, the sheltered hollow and their own urgent need for each other.

Only when he released his grip on her back and plunged his right hand down the neck of her blouse did she come to her senses. His touch was unbearably exciting, making both her nipples rise into hard, aroused peaks and sending thrills of desire through her. But it was outside her previous experience and it shocked her back to sanity.

'No!' she whimpered, grabbing at his wrist and pulling it away. 'No...don't!'

His features swam in and out of her disordered senses. She was aware that she must look a sight, with her hair blowing wildly in the wind, her face flushed and her breath coming in shallow, uneven flutters. How could she have allowed such a thing when even Ray had never touched her so intimately? And how could James have attempted it? Didn't he still believe that she was on the brink of marrying his nephew? What kind of man was he to ignore every bond of loyalty and decency in pursuit of passion? Did it mean that he had fallen so violently in love with her that he would venture anything, however illicit? Or...

Her heart turned to stone as she realised that James was making no attempt to take her in his arms again.

nstead he stood looking at her with an odd, contemptuous smile on his lips. He looked both satisfied and scornful, as if she had just given him the evidence to prove some pet theory of his. Understanding dawned on her as she saw that he hadn't been carried away by passion at all. Quite the reverse. He had deliberately set up this whole situation just to demonstrate that she would never be faithful to Sam. The swine! The cold-hearted, manipulative swine!

'You realise you can't stay here any longer, don't you?' he taunted.

Then, thrusting her away, he strode off into the sand hills alone.

CHAPTER THREE

HE WAS standing by the car with his arms folded and
stony expression on his face when she finally caught u
with him. All the turbulent feelings that had buffete
her earlier had now resolved themselves into a sing
emotion. Rage.

'Did you kiss me just so that you could prove that
don't love Sam enough to marry him?' she burst out

He shrugged. His face was like a rigid mask, with r
sign of life apart from the burning eyes and the twiste
smile.

'It hardly needs proving, does it?' he drawled insul
ingly. 'From the first moment I set eyes on you I kne
that you wanted me and that you didn't want Sar
Kissing you merely confirmed it. Frankly, I think it
despicable to marry a man you don't want just f
security.'

Laura clenched her fists so tightly that her nails t
into her palms.

'Any more despicable than trying to seduce yo
nephew's bride?' she whipped back.

His head jerked up as if she had hit him.

'I had no intention of seducing you!'

'Really? What have you just been engaged in, the
Target practice for the next lucky woman?'

'Don't be a fool. Of course I desire you. You have
very sensual presence, as you must know perfectly we
But the fact that I want you is as meaningless as the fa
that you want me. It's good, old-fashioned animal lus

54

nothing more. I would never have taken you to bed, Beatrice. When you finally commit the ultimate betrayal against Sam, it won't be with me. Some other man can have the honour.'

The sneer in his tone made Laura grit her teeth in helpless fury. She had always thought of herself as quiet and sensible, but now she felt a red-hot urge to run at James and slap his face. Her legs began to shake so much that she felt as if they would no longer hold her.

'You brute,' she breathed. 'I despise you.'

He smiled contemptuously.

'Then we're even, because I despise you too, sweetheart. And, under the circumstances, I feel it's impossible for you to remain at my home. You'll have to leave, and the sooner the better. I suggest you stay at a hotel in Hobart until the wedding—if you're still fool enough to plan on having a wedding. Naturally I'll pay for your accommodation.'

Laura contemplated trying to explain that she wasn't the one getting married, but her urge to set the record straight was immediately obliterated by a passionate thirst for revenge. James despised her, did he? Then why should she make matters any easier for him by telling him the truth? Let him go on thinking that she was Bea! It would only make him look more of a fool when he finally did find out about their deception.

And Laura wanted James to look a fool! She wanted him to suffer just as badly as he had made her suffer. Perhaps, if he felt like a complete idiot, he wouldn't even come to the wedding and she need never set eyes on him again. Fine! In any case, she certainly wasn't staying around here to be humiliated any further!

'I'd rather go back to Sydney,' she snapped.

'That's not a bad idea,' he agreed coldly. 'I'll organise a hire car for you and, if you set off immediately, you may get to Devonport in time to catch tonight's ferry. You do drive, I take it?'

'Yes.'

The journey to the north-west coast of the island was a nightmare. At first Laura felt nothing but heartfelt relief at escaping the chaos she had left behind. Yet as mile after mile slipped away, and she went over and over the events of the last two days, resentment began to engulf her, like a raging inferno.

She barely noticed the baby lambs, the pink spring blossom, the faint mist of green leaves on the willows along the creek beds or the yellow-flowered gorse bushes and clumps of spring daffodils. All she could see was James's silent, gloating face, and all she could feel was the way her fingers itched to slap it. Even when she finally went aboard the ferry and the green fields were replaced by flocks of shrieking seagulls and the vast, shimmering expanse of Bass Strait, she still could not settle. All night she lay awake in her comfortable bunk, feeling the vibration of the ship's engines and wishing she could murder Sam's uncle.

At least the long drive from Melbourne to Sydney had a hypnotic effect that was almost therapeutic. For hour after hour she sent the car hurtling up the highway, until at last exhaustion began to blunt the fury she was feeling. Even so, there were times when she was tempted to scream out loud. It struck her as a huge irony that the only time in her life she had ever met a man who made her burn with sexual passion he had to be an utter swine whom she absolutely hated.

Well, at least she only had to see him one more time, at Bea's wedding, and after that she need never set eyes on him again. She could go back to her sane, peaceful life as a career woman and congratulate herself on all she had missed. All the anger and quarrelling and insecurity of being involved with a man. No, thanks! she thought wildly. I'd rather have my job and my tidy little flat and weekend tennis rosters with Ray... Then why did her job and the tennis club suddenly seem so unutterably colourless and dreary? What had happened to her?

It was nearly eleven o'clock at night when she finally staggered in the door of her flat in Rose Bay, wanting only to crawl into her bed and die. To her annoyance she found Bea sitting on her sofa, eating popcorn and watching a video. With a gasp of outrage Laura dropped her bag, marched across to the remote control, turned off the video recorder, snatched the bowl of popcorn, took it out to the kitchen and emptied it into the garbage disposal, then stormed back to the front door and held it wide open.

'Leave before I kill you!' she snapped, pointing down the stairwell.

Bea's eyes widened incredulously.

'Laura, what's the matter with you?'

'I've just wrecked my entire life to please you, you selfish little fool, and all you can do is sit here and watch videos and drop popcorn all over my floor. Go away, will you? Just go away! And never, ever ask me to do anything for you again!'

With a bemused expression, Bea tossed one final kernel of popcorn into her mouth, licked her fingers, then craftily shut the front door and leaned against it.

'Poor Laura,' she said sympathetically. 'Was it awful?'

'It was hideous—absolutely hideous,' seethed Laura.

'Tell me about it,' invited Bea, patting her soothingly on the shoulder.

'No,' snapped Laura, jerking away from her touch. 'I don't want to talk about it. And what are you doing here anyway? Haven't you got a flat and a fiancé of your own? Or has Sam thrown you out? I don't blame him if he has.'

Bea giggled.

'Of course he hasn't! Look, Laura, why don't you take your shoes off and lie down on the sofa, and I'll make you a cup of tea while you tell me what happened in Tasmania?'

Laura looked at Bea, assessing her chances of physically wrestling her out of the front door and pushing her down the stairs, and grumpily decided against it. With a haunted expression, she allowed Bea to lead her back into the sitting room. After two aspirin and a pot of Earl Grey tea, and with a rug over her legs and a pile of cushions at her back, her feeling of hysteria subsided slightly.

'You're a wretch, Bea,' she grumbled. 'But I suppose I'm stuck with you. What happened in court? Did you get what you deserve—a ninety-nine-year sentence with hard labour?'

Bea's eyes danced.

'Nope. I was acquitted. Sam got me a really good lawyer.'

'I'm glad to hear it,' said Laura sourly. 'So what are you doing here?'

'Well, I heard you were on your way home, so I came round to find out what had happened while you were away.'

'What do you mean, you heard I was on my way home?'

'Sam rang James this morning, hoping to talk to you, and all James said was that Bea was on her way back to Sydney. He sounded pretty shirty and he hung up before we could find out anything. We're flying down there tomorrow, so I just wanted to know what we're going to walk into.'

'Did you say "flying"?' echoed Laura in disbelief.

'Yes, flying, but not on our own little wings, Laura,' explained Bea patiently. 'On a plane. The strike's over now. Hadn't you heard? It only lasted forty-eight hours.'

'Forty-eight hours,' groaned Laura. 'Just long enough to ruin my life.'

'What on earth are you talking about?'

'Nothing,' said Laura hastily. Although Bea was very sweet and affectionate, there was no way she wanted to discuss her complicated feelings about James with her. Anyway, Bea had always thought she was completely calm and self-possessed, and Laura wanted her to go on thinking that. She couldn't bear the humiliation of revealing what a fool she had been.

'Listen,' chirped Bea, 'I've got a suggestion to make. Why don't you take some more holiday leave from your job and fly back to Tasmania with us tomorrow?'

Laura almost leapt off the sofa in horror.

'Go back to Tasmania? Are you crazy? Why should I?'

Bea flashed her a guilty smile.

'So you can help me face the music with mean old Uncle James,' she said coaxingly. 'So we can own up together and tell him what bad girls we've been. Please, Laura.'

For once Bea's mischievous charm left Laura totally unmoved. In fact, she felt as if a lump of lead had settled in the pit of her stomach.

'No, Bea,' she said soberly. 'This time you've got to do it on your own, and you'd better do it soon. Because, unless I know for sure that you've told James the whole truth and made him promise to be polite to me at the wedding, I'm not even coming to it.'

Bea stared at her in horror.

'Not come to my wedding? But, Laura, you're my bridesmaid. You're my sister. You're my best friend. You're the only person in the world I care about apart from Sam. You've got to come!'

Tears sprang into Bea's eyes and her voice rang completely sincere, without the breathy little-girl undertones. For a moment Laura was tempted to weaken, then her outrage came to her aid.

'I mean it, Bea,' she warned. 'Either you fix things up with Sam's uncle, or I won't be at the wedding.'

The next few days passed with agonising slowness for Laura. Pride wouldn't allow her to telephone Bea in Tasmania, but she felt a mounting sense of desperation as time dragged by without any word from her sister. Had Bea owned up yet or not? Was James so angry that he had decided to boycott the wedding completely? She wished he would! Then she wouldn't have to suffer the humiliation of meeting his eyes in the church and remembering how he had kissed her just to prove his own cynical theories about women.

She could have forgiven him if she had felt that love or even uncontrollable attraction had prompted his actions. But the knowledge that it had all been just a game to him made her writhe with embarrassment. She hated him—hated him! Not only for what he had done to her, but for his blind prejudice against Bea. It would be a miracle if his hostility to both of them didn't blight the wedding completely.

As time dragged by, without any news, Laura found that she had trouble sleeping at night and that she couldn't concentrate at work during the day. Even Raymond noticed her preoccupation, although he put it down to excitement over his proposal of marriage.

'Oh, Laura,' he said indulgently one afternoon, shaking his head over her spreadsheets. 'You're just not with it at the moment, are you? I suppose you're flustered at getting an offer of marriage when you'd already given up hope. I'm not surprised it's taking you time to get adjusted to the idea. After all, it will mean big changes—selling your flat and that sort of thing. What you really need is some time off to think about it. Why don't you take some holiday leave so that you can get your daydreaming done out of office hours?'

Laura stared at him in baffled incomprehension. Was Ray incredibly thick and she had just never noticed it before? Or were all men so conceited that they simply couldn't believe any woman would reject their proposals of marriage? Her phone call refusing his offer didn't seem to have made any impact on Ray whatsoever! Well, she didn't feel equal to the task of trying to bludgeon the message into him again when she had so much else on her mind. And some time alone to sort out her disturbed feelings seemed like a very good idea.

'Maybe I will,' she said slowly. 'I'll get the leave forms today.'

She was sitting in her living room that evening, filling them out, when the long-awaited telephone call from Bea finally arrived. As the phone shrilled Laura jumped up and snatched the receiver.

'Laura?'

'Bea! What took you so long? What happened? Did you tell James the truth?'

There was a moment's silence and then Bea's voice came down the line, sounding unusually subdued.

'Yes, I did. But he was really angry, Laura. He couldn't see the funny side of it at all. That's why I didn't ring you earlier. Still, he's calmed down a bit now and he says...he says he'll be nice to you at the wedding and he's sorry if he upset you while you were here. So please come and be my bridesmaid!'

Laura bit her lip, feeling disconcerted. She could not suppress a twinge of satisfaction at the message that James was sorry for upsetting her, although his apology surprised her. But if he could be gracious, so could she. Perhaps she ought to speak to him now and set things on the right footing—cool, courteous and civilised. She took a long, slow breath, squared her shoulders and put on her glasses, as if she were preparing to deal with a difficult client at work.

'May I speak to him?' she asked.

'He's not here right now,' said Bea, and the strained note in her voice was more obvious than ever. 'I think he's avoiding me, actually. But I'm sure it will all be sorted out soon. Now, look, you are coming to the wedding, aren't you?'

'All right,' sighed Laura, giving in. 'I don't really want to miss it. But is it best if I try to stay out of James's way as much as possible?'

'Oh, absolutely! Actually it's lucky that you decided you wanted to stay in rented accommodation instead of with one of Sam's cousins. It makes it all so much easier.

I'll tell you what. Why don't you try and arrive Friday evening and I'll come over and see that you're settled in your cottage? Then you needn't see James at all until the wedding the following day. How does that sound?'

'All right,' agreed Laura slowly.

This time, as the rugged hills and forests of Tasmania appeared beneath the wing of the plane, Laura had a pleasant feeling of familiarity about the journey. And as she drove from the airport up the east coast she couldn't help admiring the lonely white beaches fringed by jade-green ocean, the patchwork fields, the stone cottages and dusty country roads winding up into the hills.

Only on the Saturday morning when she was dressing in her bridesmaid's frock did the first twinge of doubt attack her. What if James really hadn't changed his attitude to her? Or what if her own antagonism blazed up? Were they really capable of behaving in a civilised, restrained fashion towards each other? Or was she heading into the eye of an emotional cyclone? Still, there was no point borrowing trouble! All she could do was to concentrate on the job in hand, which was helping the bride get ready.

Bea had chosen to stay overnight with Sam's aunt, so that the bridegroom wouldn't see her in her wedding dress before the ceremony. Consequently Laura was spared the ordeal of having to confront James just yet. Instead she drove to his sister's house, where she found total chaos.

James's sister proved to be in her early thirties, with the same black hair and tawny eyes as her brother, but where James radiated purpose and energy, Wendy seemed endearingly scatty. Her cottage—'Only a weekender. I'm a lawyer in Launceston, Monday to Friday.'—

was littered with books, clothes, unwashed plates, Labrador dogs and young men. Fortunately she and Bea seemed to be firm friends already, which Laura found comforting. It was nice to think Bea would have an ally who could defend her from James's disapproval once Laura had left for Sydney.

As she helped Bea into her long gown of ivory silk she felt a twinge of sadness. Soon Bea would belong to the Fraser family, while she would be more alone than ever. Well, she shouldn't begrudge her sister's good fortune. Better to concentrate on how gorgeous she, Laura, was going to look in her own red bridesmaid's frock and how much fun she would have at the reception.

When the first of the wedding cars arrived to take her to the church, she kissed Bea's cold cheek and squeezed her hand.

'Good luck. I suppose James will be here in about five minutes to pick you up. We'll, I'll see you both at the church.'

'Bye, Laura. Good luck to you too.'

Arriving in the church, Laura felt as strung up as if it were her own wedding, and she flushed crimson when the vicar came to meet her in the porch and frowned severely at her.

'Beatrice told me all about your little escapade,' he said in a stage whisper. 'You're wicked girls, the pair of you. I haven't had such goings-on in my church since Sam and John Timmins drank the communion wine when they were twelve years old. I hope you're both thoroughly ashamed of yourselves.'

Laura bit her lip, suppressed a violent urge to giggle and nodded penitently. Bill Archer pinched her on the cheek.

'Good. Well, let's get on with the service.'

He went back into the vestry and Laura stole a peep at the inside of the church, which was rapidly filling up with guests. Nearly all of them were Sam's friends and relations. It was only because she and Bea were alone in the world that her sister had chosen to be married in this place that meant so much to her bridegroom. Laura felt an involuntary pang of envy at the sight of that tiny church packed to capacity with so many well-wishers. Not that she regretted her own single status for an instant, but there were moments when she couldn't help wishing...

She left the thought unfinished as the sound of a car pulling up on the gravel turning circle alerted her to the arrival of the bride. Not only the bride. James would be in that car too, since he was taking the place of Beatrice's father. Laura's palms grew suddenly clammy and her heart began to beat violently as she walked towards the car to help Bea out with her long train. Bea emerged looking beautiful, but Laura's gaze was transfixed on the tall, masculine figure in a morning coat and striped trousers stepping out of the other side of the car. She stared at him in bewilderment.

'Peter Clark!' she blurted out. 'But where's James?'

'I'm sorry, Laura,' said Bea. 'There's something I didn't tell you—'

She got no further, for at that moment another car pulled up on the gravel and a second man stepped out of it. He too was dressed in a morning coat and striped trousers, but there the resemblance ended. Where Peter Clark was grey-haired, red-faced and cheerful-looking, the newcomer was lean, dark and visibly grim. He strode across the gravel with a face like thunder, and then stopped in his tracks as if he had been shot.

'Beatrice,' he said, looking straight at Laura. 'What the hell is going on here? Why are you dressed in a bridesmaid's outfit? And if you're the bridesmaid, who on earth is the bride?'

Laura felt a cold, sick feeling trickle through her limbs as she realised the truth. Obviously Bea hadn't confessed to him after all! But why? Why?

'I'm not Bea, I'm Laura,' she croaked.

James stared at her as if she had taken leave of her senses.

'What do you mean? What's going on here?'

Out of the corner of her eye Laura saw a blur of white. She swung round just in time to catch Bea creeping off towards the church and grabbed her sister ruthlessly by the arm.

'Yes, what is going on here?' she demanded.

'Sorry,' babbled Bea, turning back to face them with a nervous smile on her lips, 'I guess I forgot to tell you, Laura. For some reason James went off in a huff after your visit and left a note saying he wasn't coming to the wedding. Well, I really didn't tell you because I was afraid you wouldn't come either. But now that you're both here, I suppose that we should introduce ourselves. I'm Bea, she's Laura, you must be James. I'm the bride, she's the bridesmaid, you're giving me away. Now, let's get started, shall we?'

With a stunned expression, James allowed Bea to seize his arm and lead him into the porch of the church. There she stopped and smiled radiantly at the sexton.

'You don't mind, do you, Peter?'

Peter, looking even more dazed than James, shook his head and then lumbered into the church to join the rest of the guests. Torn between shock, disbelief and pure, murderous rage, Laura followed her sister inside and picked up the silk train. But as the 'Bridal March' echoed from the organ she had eyes only for James, who was casting her glances of baffled fury over his shoulder. Good. Well, let him suffer! He deserved it, didn't he?

Still, she would have liked to wring Bea's neck. She had come here believing that all the unpleasantness had been smoothed over and that James understood their masquerade. Instead it looked as though there was going to be a real lulu of a scene in front of a hundred fascinated wedding guests when he demanded the inevitable explanations. Laura cringed inwardly at the thought and tried to drag her wandering attention back to the wedding.

Somehow she managed to blunder down the aisle in Bea's wake, but she felt as disorientated as if she were trapped in a dream. She was dimly aware of the expectant faces turned towards them, of Sam looking tall and rugged and beaming from ear to ear as Beatrice glided towards him, of the vicar gaping in dismay at the sight of James scowling beside the bride. Yet most of her own attention was taken up by the turmoil raging inside her. Why hadn't Beatrice told her the truth? Why had James gone away after she'd left Tasmania? And what was he doing here now? She stole another glance at him and saw that he was staring at her, with his tawny eyes narrowed so that the pupils were nothing but dark, angry dots. The words of the service echoed in her head.

'Holy Matrimony...is an honourable estate...not by any to be enterprised, nor taken in hand, unadvisedly, lightly, or wantonly, to satisfy men's carnal lusts...but reverently, discreetly, advisedly, soberly...'

A sudden flash of memory assaulted her and she found herself transported back to the beach, with James's arms tightened around her and his burning kisses raining down on her. There had been nothing discreet or sober about that! Her cheeks flamed at the memory, and from the knowing flash in his eyes she guessed that he knew what she was thinking. Suddenly the church seemed suffocating, with its smell of flowers and candles, its press of human bodies. Laura longed to rush outside, to race over the hills and hide, but as she saw the way James's hands were clenched at his sides, she knew that there would be no escape.

When at last the service came to an end and an ecstatic bridal couple followed the vicar into the vestry, with Laura, James, Sam's parents and the best man in procession behind them, she realised with a sinking sensation that the reckoning was nigh. James stood in smouldering silence as John and Laura witnessed the signatures in the registry.

'And now the photos!' cried Bea rapturously.

'You can do without Laura and me for five minutes,' growled James. 'Go on, all of you. Out!'

'My dear friend,' began the vicar, 'let there be no violence in the—'

'You heard me. Out!'

There was a buzz of speculation inside the church as the incomplete procession made its way back between the pews, but the sound was cut off by the ominous slam of the heavy oak door. James leaned against the solid wood and treated Laura to a long, contemptuous appraisal. Every muscle in his body radiated danger, and there was something alarming in the steady rise and fall of his chest as he breathed and in the strangely predatory tension in his shoulders. He looked like a panther preparing to spring.

'All right, what's going on?' he hissed. 'Why did you lie to me?'

She winced at the blatant hostility in his voice and moistened her lips.

'It was just a harmless deception . . .' she faltered.

'Harmless?' To her alarm he suddenly crossed the vestry in two strides and pinned her against the sandstone wall. She gasped as he seized her shoulders and her heart began to hammer violently at the sight of his contorted features thrust so close to hers. 'Do you call that harmless—the sort of chaos that you and your sister have perpetrated in the last week? What was it all about? Answer me!'

She flinched at his scathing tone, but raised her head defiantly.

'Bea asked me to come down and take her place last week when she was supposed to look over the house in Hobart.'

'Why?'

The curt monosyllable echoed round the room like the crack of a whiplash.

'Because she was in trouble,' said Laura with a defeated sigh. 'She had to go to court to be charged with a traffic offence and she thought you would be shocked if you knew the truth. She also thought you'd be offended if she didn't show up to see the house, so she asked me to come and pretend I was her. I wasn't really happy about it, but it seemed quite harmless. You weren't even supposed to be there and I didn't think you'd ever know we'd swapped places.'

'That doesn't excuse a blatant piece of deceit,' he snarled. 'Once I did arrive, you should have told me the truth immediately. Instead you let me think you were my nephew's bride. Your behaviour was outrageous.'

Her guilt gave way to an uprush of anger.

'Any more outrageous than yours?' she countered. 'I seem to remember that you had an interesting way of welcoming your nephew's bride to the family acres!'

He flushed at that, and Laura had the satisfaction of knowing she had scored a direct hit. But instead of defending his own behaviour, or apologising for it, he went on the attack once more.

'Why didn't you tell me the truth immediately?'

'Because Bea phoned and begged me not to. I promised I'd leave it up to her to tell you.'

He gave a ferocious growl of laughter.

'She certainly chose her moment, didn't she? Waiting until the wedding day and making me look a complete fool! Or was that your inspiration?'

'No! After I went back to Sydney I made Bea promise that she would tell you before the wedding. She said she had, but she must have lied. I suppose she lost her nerve.'

'Possibly not,' James admitted grudgingly. 'I haven't been here ever since you left. She wouldn't have had a chance to speak to me until now.'

Laura shot him a puzzled look.

'Where did you go?' she demanded.

His face was cold and inscrutable, revealing nothing. 'I went out to an offshore island where I keep some sheep. There's no telephone there.'

She was silent for a moment, bewildered by this unexpected revelation. What had driven him away? Embarrassment? A belated feeling of guilt towards Sam for making advances to his supposed fiancée? Or had he simply taken such a violent dislike to Laura herself that he hadn't wanted to set eyes on her again?

'Why did you go?' she asked thoughtfully. 'Was it just routine work, or...?'

His reply took her completely by surprise.

'I found that I didn't much fancy the thought of watching you marry another man,' he said coldly. 'Even my nephew. Especially my nephew.'

Laura was stunned. What did this mean? Could it possibly mean that he had felt a genuine liking for her and not just an involuntary physical attraction?

'Then why did you come back?' she asked warily.

James shrugged.

'Blame it on my sense of duty! I'm supposed to be the rational one in the family. It didn't seem very rational to let my animal lust for you override my loyalty to Sam.'

Animal lust. The words ripped through her like bullets, wounding her to the core. There was no mistaking the cynicism in his eyes as he gazed coldly back at her. No, James Fraser hadn't liked her one bit. He had merely been trying to prove that all women were fickle and that he could have any one of them whenever he chose. She tried to hide her hurt by lashing back at him.

'I'm so pleased to know that you're motivated by loyalty to Sam,' she purred. 'It must have been such a relief when you realised today that I was only the bridesmaid and not his bride.'

His eyes glinted dangerously.

'It was. And I'm glad to know what you really are at last.' His tone had been unmistakably jeering as he'd spoken the words 'what you really are'. Did he mean that now he knew she was a cheat and a liar? Before she could ask him point blank, he continued. 'Well, now that we've got all that sorted out, shall we go back and rejoin this farcical ceremony? Perhaps we can even have a photo together, as a memento of an unforgettable occasion.'

Seizing her hand as if she were a particularly defiant kindergarten child, he opened the door and hustled her through the rapidly emptying church to the front porch. There was a buzz of comment and several people darted curious glances from James's tight-lipped features to her defiant ones as they joined the rest of the wedding party.

Although she yearned for the ground to open and swallow her up, Laura was determined not to ruin Bea's wedding, and she did her best to smile as the photographer's flash blazed. Fortunately Bea seemed oblivious of any tension and looked absolutely radiant as she flung her arms around the pair of them and drew them into a photo just with her and Sam.

'You've been such a good sport about this!' she trilled, standing on tiptoes and kissing James resoundingly. 'I'm so glad you don't bear grudges.'

James gave her a cold look and Laura cringed inwardly. She couldn't entirely blame him for being annoyed, and yet she also felt an unexpected surge of anger at the way he was spurning Bea's peace overtures. Couldn't he see how well-meaning and harmless and affectionate her sister was? Did he really intend to hold a permanent grudge against her from now on? Well, at least Laura herself didn't have to have any more to do with him!

But first there was the reception to endure. This was to be held in an old sandstone hotel only a stone's throw from the church, and Laura enjoyed a few moments' respite in the soothing task of holding up Bea's train as they walked across to the other building. Once inside the gracious ballroom, with its parquetry floor, high ceiling and long windows overlooking the water, Laura found her reprieve was over. A stylishly dressed auburn-haired woman in her mid-forties marched briskly across to her, extended her gloved hand and spoke in a high, carrying voice.

'How do you do? You must be Laura and I'm Priscilla, Sam's mother. I'm so sorry we didn't have a chance to meet before the ceremony. However, since you and dear Beatrice haven't any parents of your own, I've arranged for you and James to take the place of the bride's parents in the receiving line. Come along, now. I want you standing by the door. You're to shake hands with everyone who comes in, then pass them on to Adrian and me and finally to the bride and groom.'

With a sinking sensation, Laura found herself pushed into position next to James and moved around to Priscilla's satisfaction. James seemed to derive a certain sardonic amusement from his ex-sister-in-law's manoeuvres, and endured her fussing with an expression of lazy derision.

'Priscilla's father was a major in the Australian Army,' he remarked when at last she moved away.

He hadn't bothered to drop his voice and Laura saw a militant flash in the older woman's eyes as she took her place a few feet away from them. Not wanting to trigger off a family row, she ducked her head and mumbled something inaudible. Wasn't a wedding supposed to be the happiest day of a woman's life? Well, it didn't look as if Bea's was going completely to plan! What with the icy civility between Sam's divorced parents and the Cold War between Laura and James, she would be lucky if she didn't have a massacre on her hands by the end of the day.

'Mr and Mrs William Evans,' announced the usher.

The line of guests began to move forward and Laura forced herself to smile, although a turbulent whirlpool of feelings was seething inside her.

She only had to look at Bea's starry eyes and the glow in Sam's rugged face to feel absurdly glad about the whole event, so glad that she almost wanted to burst into tears of joy. Yet along with her happiness went an aching sense of loneliness. Things would never be the same for her and Bea from now on. It was odd to think that Bea was married and she wasn't. In fact, walking up the aisle as a substitute bride at a wedding rehearsal was probably the closest she would ever get to being married herself. Unless she married Raymond. The thought depressed her so much that she heaved a deep sigh. James's hand tightened warningly on her arm.

'Try to look cheerful, can't you?' he whispered. 'Anyone would think you were at a funeral, not a wedding.'

His criticism annoyed her, but she had to admit the justice of the warning. With a determined effort, she pinned a smile on her lips and held out her hand as the usher announced the next couple.

'Captain and Mrs Charles Russell.'

Most of the guests were friendly and welcoming, although a few flashed covert glances from her to James as the line crawled forward. Once she heard the whisper 'swapped places' followed by 'Shh!' and felt her cheeks burn, but she held her head high and forced herself to continue shaking hands. Only once did her composure falter, when the usher announced 'Mrs Sue Rigby' and a blonde woman of about thirty stepped forward to shake hands with them both. Something in the way the woman's eyes met James's set warning bells clamouring in Laura's head and she looked more attentively at the guest.

To her dismay she saw that the other woman had the sort of slender, petite grace that made Laura feel like a raw-boned peasant in comparison. Sue's clothes were impressive too—an exquisitely tailored dress in jade-green silk, with a toning floral jacket, complemented by a gold and pearl necklace and gold earrings. Her hair was styled in a geometric cut that showed off the flawless regularity of her features, with thickly lashed green eyes under arching eyebrows, a small, straight nose and perfect teeth. Only a touch of hardness about that lovely mouth robbed her face of total perfection. But James didn't seem to have any complaints. Something in the intimate way he smiled down at Sue made Laura's skin prickle with disapproval.

'Where's Mr Rigby?' she asked in a stage whisper once the other woman was safely out of earshot.

'Away in the Navy,' replied James carelessly.

Once the receiving line had ended, the gathering became more informal as white-jacketed waiters moved around with trays of champagne and savouries. Rather to Laura's relief, James deserted her at the first possible opportunity and began to move about the room, talking to friends and relations. She realised she ought to be doing the same thing, as the only bridesmaid, but there didn't seem any pressing need for her to oil the wheels socially. Everybody else knew each other—anyway, her feet were hurting and she felt thoroughly depressed.

Picking up a glass of champagne, she sneaked behind a potted palm and sat down with a sigh of relief in an empty Chippendale chair. Yet, in spite of all her good resolutions, she could not prevent herself from watching James's progress around the room. He did seem to have good manners; she had to give him that. If she hadn't still been smarting because of their recent clash, she would have admired the way he moved easily from group to group, chatting to everyone.

She was just watching him restore a crying child to her mother, when her attention was distracted by a flurry of movement in the chair next to her. She turned just in time to see Sam's Aunt Wendy kick off her shoes with a sigh of relief and take a hefty gulp of champagne. Wendy grinned at her and raised her glass in a toast.

'Well, here's to you, Laura, I really have to hand it to you. You're the first woman I've seen in fourteen years who's managed to get under my brother's skin. James is absolutely furious with you.'

'Furious?' echoed Laura in bewilderment, her gaze scanning the room in search of him. 'I thought he seemed completely calm.'

'That's when he's at his most dangerous! Take it from me, he would love to murder you. In fact, I doubt if he'll ever forgive you for what you and Bea did.'

Laura winced.

'Oh, don't,' she begged. 'I already feel guilty enough about it. It was an awful thing to do.'

'Rubbish! It will do him good. After all, he's been making women suffer enough for the last fourteen years. Let him try it for a change.'

Laura felt a reluctant stir of curiosity.

'What do you mean, "making women suffer"?'

Wendy settled more comfortably into her chair with the air of someone preparing for a good gossip. She leaned forward confidentially.

'His wife Paula treated him pretty badly, and after she left I think he must have sworn some kind of vow that he was going to take his revenge on females in general.'

'Revenge? Why, what does he do?' asked Laura.

'He seems to specialise in enticing women into falling for him and then abandoning them. Or that's the way it looks to an unbiased observer. Ever since he got divorced there have been heaps of women who hoped he would marry them, but he never does. He's absolutely

famous for being attentive and charming until he's really
lured them in, and then he loses interest and drops them.
Look at him going to work on Sue Rigby over there.'

Laura jerked her head up hastily, just in time to see
James taking two glasses of champagne from a waiter's
tray and handing one of them to Sue with a caressing
gesture. With their heads very close together, they
chinked glasses and then drank in some kind of private
toast.

'Isn't he a bastard?' continued Wendy admiringly.
'Mind you, most of the women he's ditched have deserved it, in my opinion, and you never know, Sue might
just prove to be the exception and catch him unawares.
She's famous for getting what she wants. Oh, excuse me,
I've just seen a really luscious man going to waste with
my dreary cousin. I'll catch you later.'

Retrieving her shoes, Wendy rose to her feet and
moved purposefully away, leaving Laura with plenty to
ponder. Was James really as callous as his sister suggested? And, if so, what business was it of hers? She
wasn't going to have any more to do with him, was she?
All she felt for him was dislike of his arrogance, and
there was no doubt that the antagonism was mutual. He
had already made it perfectly clear that the only thing
he felt towards her was hostility.

Throughout the rest of the wedding reception Laura
had no reason to change that opinion. James certainly
didn't seem to be making any attempt to add her to his
tally of conquests. The few remarks he addressed to her
over the meal were all completely harmless and, although
he did invite her to dance once when the band began
playing, she felt sure that it was only out of duty. And,
when the best man proposed the toast to the bridesmaid,

she noticed that James tossed off his champagne as if he were drinking some kind of vile medicine.

She was relieved when the time came for her to go upstairs and help her sister change for her departure. When Bea was finally ready, and looking ravishing in a red woollen suit, she gave Laura a rapturous hug.

'I'm so glad you came! It made everything perfect, and I know James will be nice to you from now on. Listen, couldn't you stay on here a bit longer and have a holiday? I'm sure he'd be glad to show you around.'

Laura thought of the hostility that had smouldered between her and James throughout the reception and she shook her head at Bea's unquenchable optimism.

'I don't think so,' she said.

Which made it all the more of a shock when James approached her after Sam and Bea's car had roared away and posed an offhand question.

'Why don't you stay on at my place for a while?' he asked. 'I think we ought to get to know each other.'

CHAPTER FOUR

LAURA was so taken aback that she could only gape at him, but his face was inscrutable and gave little clue to the motives that lay behind his invitation. Was it a genuine attempt at peacemaking or...? Something in the hooded stillness of his tawny gaze sent a shiver of apprehension up her spine. No, she didn't think that peacemaking was high on James Fraser's agenda, and his sister's blunt warning suddenly echoed in her head with ominous significance. 'He seems to specialise in enticing women into falling for him and then abandoning them.' Was that what he was up to? Well, if so, she wasn't going to be one of his guinea pigs!

'That's very kind of you,' she said with an unconvincing smile. 'But I'm afraid I'll have to refuse. I have other plans.'

He shrugged.

'What a pity. You and I have a lot to discuss. Are you sure you won't change your mind?'

'Quite sure.'

An absurd pang of regret stabbed through her as he smiled carelessly and moved away to speak to somebody else. With a feeling of anticlimax she made her own rounds of the remaining guests, shaking hands and uttering mechanical farewells. She felt a momentary flicker of pleasure when Wendy also urged her to stay on for a few days' sightseeing, but with some regret she refused that invitation too. There was far too much risk of running into James if she was at his sister's house.

All the same, her disappointment lingered until Wendy dropped her off at the colonial cottage where she was staying. But as she pushed open the bedroom door disappointment was abruptly transformed into complete bewilderment at the discovery that the owner of the cottage was busy making up the bed with fresh sheets. Not only that, but all Laura's possessions had vanished. What on earth was going on?

'What are you doing?' asked Laura. 'And where's all my luggage?'

'Goodness, you startled me!' said the woman, rising to her feet and shaking a pillow into a clean pillowslip. 'James Fraser came a few minutes ago and collected your bags. He said you were going to stay at his house for a while. Has there been some mistake?'

Rage scorched through Laura's veins like neat alcohol. There certainly has, she thought to herself. She opened her mouth to pour out her indignation and then paused. The other woman was looking at her with avid curiosity, and the realisation dawned on her that she had probably already heard the story of how Laura and Bea had swapped places at the wedding rehearsal. The last thing Laura wanted to do was fuel any more small town gossip. With an effort she controlled herself.

'No—o,' she said slowly. 'Not really. It's just that James has moved faster than I expected. I, um, didn't think I'd be going to his place until tomorrow. Well, I suppose the only thing to do is to settle up my account and go and have a talk to good old James about this.'

'Oh, there's nothing to pay,' said the other woman brightly, smoothing the bedspread over the pillows. 'James has already settled your account.'

Laura gritted her teeth.

'I see. Well, thank you very much. I've enjoyed my stay here.'

'Good. Perhaps you'll come and visit us another time.'

'Perhaps.'

Laura was so furious that she sent the hire car hurtling along the country roads, raising a cloud of gravel and fawn dust as she went. When at last she pulled up outside James's farmhouse, she marched in through the open back door and then paused in the hallway, looking about her. A thudding sound led her to the dining room, where she found James on his knees at the hearth, stirring up a blazing fire with a poker. He turned at her approach, rose to his feet and smiled. It was an infuriating smile—smug, sly and full of triumphant amusement. It made Laura's blood boil.

'What are you playing at?' she snapped.

'I could ask you the same thing,' he replied lazily. 'I don't think we've got our accounts entirely settled yet, do you? I want to talk to you.'

'So that's why you've stolen my luggage and paid my bill without asking me?' she flared. 'I could sue you for this.'

'Could you?' he replied mildly. 'Is it a criminal offence to pay someone's bill? I must ask Wendy.'

'Well, if it's not an offence, it should be! Will you kindly tell me how much I owe you, give me my bags and let me go?'

James's smile grew broader.

'No.'

'What do you mean—no?'

'Exactly what I say. I want you to stay and have tea with me, Laura, so that we can have a little talk.' He gestured at the table, which was invitingly set with fine china and an array of cakes and biscuits. 'It's all ready.'

'I don't want tea,' snapped Laura, although as a matter of fact she was dying for a cup. 'I want to get my bags and go back and stay at the cottage where I was before you interfered.'

'Oh, that won't be possible, I'm afraid,' said James, shaking his head regretfully. 'It's already been let to someone else for the night.'

'How do you know?'

'Well, when I told Cathy Wace that you were staying here with me, I also suggested to my cousin Bill Evans and his wife that they might like to stay there overnight instead of driving home. And I think you'll find every other place around here is booked out because of the wedding. That seems to leave you with a choice of staying with me or facing a long drive to Hobart in your brides-maid's dress without any luggage.'

Laura stared at him in horrified comprehension.

'Do you mean you're refusing to hand over my luggage unless I stay here?'

James remained silent, but his eyebrows rose sar-donically and a taunting smile remained glued to his lips. He made the faintest possible inclination of his head, which might have been a nod.

'You can't do that!' she burst out.

'Can't I?'

That smoky, provocative voice was the last straw. Without warning, Laura lost her temper. Letting out a low gasp of rage, she stormed across the room as tem-pestuously as a river in spate, picking up obstacles and flinging them aside. She tripped over the poker and kicked it aside, snatched the Saturday newspaper off the couch and hurled that away, then dropped down into an armchair with a groan of outrage.

'It's unfair—utterly unfair!' she shouted. 'First my idiot sister drags me into this mess and then I end up in the clutches of a lunatic who steals my luggage and tries to trap me here. Well, I won't stay, do you hear me? I won't stay!'

She flung her arms wide in such a fierce gesture that her right fist knocked over a lamp, which tumbled onto the coffee-table with a loud crash. James ambled across and set it upright again.

'You know, Sam told me you were the calm, sensible one in the family,' he remarked in a conversational tone.

'Oh, shut up!' exclaimed Laura.

Kneeling down, he began to pick up a saucer full of candies which had been scattered by Laura's attack on the lamp.

'I still can't believe a mature woman like you would get involved in such a ridiculous masquerade,' he remarked.

'Do you think it was my idea?' she demanded hotly.

'Well, you didn't try to stop her, did you?'

'It would have been like trying to stop a volcano from erupting. She's uncontrollable; she always has been! I've spent eighteen years trying to head her away from disaster and it hardly ever works.'

He paused in his task and looked at her thoughtfully. Crouched down as he was, he was only a few inches away from her, and his eyes were on a level with hers. She found that steady, golden gaze unnerving, and even more unnerving was the knowledge of the latent strength in his body. He would only have to reach out and take hold of her and she would be trapped at his mercy in the armchair. The thought sent a tingling thrill of apprehension through her.

'You must have had a difficult life.'

She looked away from him, unable to meet his gaze for fear of blushing self-consciously.

'Not really,' she said shortly. 'Lots of people have been through far worse.'

'Tell me about it. You were orphans, weren't you?'

'Close enough,' she admitted. 'My parents separated when I was eight and my father went off mining in Western Australia, which was the last I ever heard of him. Then my mother developed cancer and died three years later. There were no relatives, so Bea and I—' She broke off and scowled at him. 'I don't know why I'm telling you all this.'

'Perhaps because you've never had anyone else to tell? I'll admit Beatrice seems charming, but she strikes me as pretty selfish too. You must have sacrificed a lot for her.'

For some reason the intent way that he was looking at her brought a hard lump into Laura's throat. Nobody before had ever understood or cared how much she had given up for Bea. Nobody had even noticed her next to Bea.

'I didn't begrudge it,' she said hoarsely. 'She was so little when Mum—'

Her voice broke and she couldn't go on. To her horror she found tears prickling her eyes. She bit her lip and blinked twice, vainly trying to force them back. It would have been all right if James had attacked her or baited her—she could have coped with that. But his unexpected sympathy, coming so close upon the drama of the wedding, was more than she could bear.

Without warning a muffled sob escaped her, and to her amazement James's large, warm hand closed over hers. Silently he rose to his feet, hauled her upright and engulfed her in the most comforting embrace she had ever experienced. It was like being hugged by an oak tree or a mountain, some primeval force of nature that was utterly strong and safe. Laura had never felt so protected, so cherished in her entire life.

She took an unsteady breath, luxuriating in the warmth of his touch, in the slow, regular thud of his heartbeat next to her cheek, in the powerful grip of his arms around her. Her spirits soared and an aching sense of completeness swept through her.

Could this be the man she had thought she hated? The man she had dismissed as arrogant and self-centred? Then how could he be holding her so protectively, as if he were the still and certain centre of the universe, a fixed point in a crazy, uncertain world? How could he be so kind? Had she misjudged him? I could easily fall in love with you, James, she thought wildly and was appalled by the discovery. Her eyes flew open and she gazed up at him searchingly, craving some sign that he was as shaken and perturbed by their closeness as she was.

But his face was unreadable. His eyes certainly held the glint of some powerful emotion, but what it was she couldn't guess. Perhaps it was as simple as physical lust— for he did want her; she was sure of that. Something in the tension of his muscles, the set of his mouth, the uneven rhythm of his breathing made her certain of that. But was there more than just desire? An emotional craving to match his physical hunger for her? She could not be certain.

Ashamed at her uncharacteristic display of emotion, she groped at her non-existent pockets in a vain search for a handkerchief and then found that James had pressed his into her hand. It was square and starched and unpretentious, but exactly what she needed. Sniffing convulsively, she dabbed at her eyes and made a feeble joke.

'Sorry,' she said indistinctly. 'It's the wedding. I always cry at weddings.'

'I'll bet,' he growled, then, laying one heavy hand on her shoulders, he led her across to the dining table, pushed her firmly into a seat and sat down beside her.

'You're going to have some tea and after that you're going to tell me everything about yourself,' he instructed.

Laura had thought she wasn't hungry after the huge meal at the reception, but when James went into the kitchen and returned with a pot of tea, she discovered she was wrong. The walnut shortbread, smoked salmon sandwiches and lemon cake looked too tempting to resist. Besides, the emotional roller coaster of the day's events had left her in need of restoration.

He waited until she had eaten her fill and drunk three cups of tea before he spoke again. Everything had seemed to change between them during that long silence and she was conscious of his gaze boring through her, as if he were trying to fathom what she was really like. His expression, although compassionate, was determined, and she knew he wouldn't rest until he'd learnt everything he wanted to know about her. It was disconcerting, but unexpectedly flattering to be the object of such intent scrutiny.

'Have you ever talked about your mother's death to anyone?' he demanded at last.

'Not really. I was afraid I'd go to pieces if I did and upset Bea even more. And nobody else cared.'

'I care. Tell me.'

A spasm crossed her face and she rocked backwards and forwards, biting her upper lip. Even now that long-ago grief was dangerously close to the surface.

'I might start crying again if I do.'

'It doesn't matter. I think you should talk about it.'

She dropped her gaze and began pleating the hem of the bridesmaid's frock between her fingers. Her words came haltingly.

'Well, I feel the obvious stuff. I was really sad that she died. I missed her a lot and sometimes I even felt angry with her for leaving me. I didn't think I could cope with what was ahead of me.'

'Tell me about it,' he urged. 'What happened? I know I asked you these questions last time you were here, but I'm not sure any more what your answers meant. I don't know whether you were talking about Bea or yourself. It's Laura I want to know about now.'

'Laura!' she exclaimed with a gasp of mirthless laughter. 'Boring old Laura! There's nothing worth telling. I was fostered until I was eighteen, then I went to university and qualified as an accountant, and as soon as I had a job I persuaded the welfare department to let me look after Bea. That's been my life ever since. My sister and my work.'

'Don't talk about yourself in that contemptuous tone. You ought to be proud of what you've done. I think you showed a lot of courage.'

Laura shrugged.

'Do you?' her voice was offhand, but she couldn't help feeling warmed by his obvious admiration.

'Yes, I do,' he said. Abruptly he rose to his feet and paced across to the window. 'What's more, I think you deserve a good long break after all your efforts. Your hare-brained sister and my callow nephew have managed to get married in spite of any misgivings which you or I might have about their wisdom in doing so. Well, now they're going to have to prove that they're adults and deal with any consequences that arise themselves. What that means, Laura, is that you're off the hook. You've got to stop living your life for Bea and start living it for yourself.'

He was right, but it was something she had avoided facing until now. She made a small, dismissive move with her hands, as if it were nothing important, but there was an urgency in his voice and his eyes that demanded some comment. An insistence that she face the question of what she intended to do with her life.

'I suppose so,' she admitted at last, pulling a mocking face. 'So what do you think I should do first? Rob a bank? Dance the can-can naked on Sydney Harbour Bridge? Go skydiving without a parachute? You know so much—you tell me!'

He swung round and looked at her and she saw the gleam of amusement in his eyes. Amusement and something else. Something that sent a tingling current down her spine.

'I think you should do something far more dangerous and disturbing than any of those things,' he replied in a silky voice. 'I think you should stay and spend a few weeks with me.'

It's a good thing Bea's not here, thought Laura as she drifted hazily into consciousness the following morning. She'd die laughing at the way I've given in so easily. Worse still, she might even notice that I've softened towards James. Well, at least nobody else is going to know or care, and if I'm careful I can hide it from him. I don't want any more embarrassing scenes, but why should there be any? The truth about our masquerade is out in the open now, and even if James was horrible to me at the wedding, he was really nice last night. So calm and reassuring... I'll be safe with him...

Her thoughts began to drift and she found herself sinking into sleep again, only to be confronted by the floating image of James's sister Wendy. Wendy's voice rang in her head, saying something about James being at his most dangerous when he seemed completely calm. Laura sprang up in bed with a startled cry.

'Oh, damn it!' she exclaimed, flinging back the covers and trudging across to peer at herself in the mirror above the chest of drawers. 'I don't care if he is dangerous! I'm sick of being rational and sensible anyway. Maybe it's time I took a few more risks with my life!'

James's challenge the previous evening seemed to have awoken an unfamiliar recklessness inside her, but her expression in the mirror looked so impetuous that she recoiled in alarm. Drawing back the curtains, she squinted at herself critically. Was she undergoing a complete personality transformation? Was it the sort of thing that happened to women when their last child left home? In a way, she had been almost like a mother to Bea, and now Bea had left her for ever. Could she be having a mid-life crisis at the age of twenty-nine?

'Well, if I am, I'm going to enjoy it,' she announced defiantly, striking a sexy pose and leering at herself as if she were Bea modelling black lace underwear. Of course she'd need to lost about thirty pounds before she'd look good in black lace underwear, but she enjoyed the feeling of recklessness that the thought gave her. Then her old common sense descended on her like a cold, damp blanket. 'Oh, who am I kidding? Nothing dramatic is going to happen. I'm just going to have a holiday with James. A friendly, harmless holiday!'

All the same, she could not quite control the dizzy, bubbling feeling inside her as they ate breakfast together. James was wearing jeans and an open-necked blue shirt that revealed his muscular, suntanned chest.

'Do you have anything in particular you'd like to do today?' he asked.

Laura shrugged.

'I don't really know where to start. What would you suggest?'

'Do you ride at all? I've got to go down and check on some fallow deer that I keep in an enclosure at the foot of the hill. Afterwards we could go for a ride along the beach if that appeals to you.'

'I'd love to,' said Laura wistfully. 'But I've never been on a horse in my life.'

'Then it's time you started. I've got a nice gentle mare I can put you on. Now, what about clothes? Have you got jeans and a sweater?'

'Yes, I have,' agreed Laura, 'Although that's something else I'll have to tackle before long. I've only brought enough clothes for two or three days. I don't know if—'

'That's easy. I'll take you shopping in Hobart tomorrow.'

'I can't afford—'

'You don't have to. It's an old Tasmanian bridal custom that the uncle of the groom always buys the bridesmaid some clothes immediately after the wedding.'

Laura choked on her orange juice. All the same, she couldn't help admiring his barefaced effrontery.

'Liar,' she spluttered.

'Well, we'll sort it out tomorrow. Now, get changed and we'll go riding.'

It was a glorious day, crisp and cool and sunny, and when Laura came out to the stable she found James already busy saddling the horses. Steam was rising from their damp coats in gold wisps and their breath left frosty clouds in the air. As they stamped and snorted and jingled their bridles Laura felt a wave of exhilaration, as if she were ten years old again.

'Come and I'll show you how to check that the girth is tight enough,' instructed James.

Obediently she joined him on the near side of one of the horses and let him guide her fingers under the strap that encircled the creature's warm, shaggy belly. They were standing so close together that she could feel James's arm brushing against hers and see his frosty breath stirring the air as he spoke. An involuntary thrill of excitement went through her.

When he hoisted her up into the saddle and adjusted the stirrup leathers for her, the excitement changed to panic. Suddenly the horse which had seemed so large when she was standing on the ground seemed a pitifully inadequate place to sit, while its motion was as daunting as the swaying and pitching of a ship. She tried to hide her misgivings as James clicked his tongue, dug his heels into his bay gelding's flanks and glanced encouragingly over his shoulder to her.

To her relief the mare lurched after him, and they were soon ambling down the hill towards the deer enclosure at the bottom. Here they paused and looked through the wire netting at the thirty or forty animals that were scattered around the paddock. Most were lying down or grazing peacefully, but there was a rattling noise as two young stags ran together and clashed antlers. James gave a throaty chuckle.

'Testing their virility,' he said. 'The females will only want to mate with the one who's the toughest and strongest and best able to protect them. That means learning to fight for what they want at a very early age.'

Laura pondered over his blunt words as he dismounted from the horse, hitched it to a convenient sapling and disappeared into a shed near the gateway. Within moments he emerged with a couple of bales of hay which he carried effortlessly into the enclosure and began distributing it to the deer. Watching his easy, muscular grace as he undid the twine that bound the bales and scattered the golden hay, she was struck by the way he seemed in complete harmony with his environment.

Like the animals he tended, James Fraser was earthy and primitive and in touch with his natural instincts. Perhaps it was that very quality of animal magnetism that attracted her so urgently to him. Yet if she felt that irresistible tug of excitement in his presence, wouldn't other women experience it equally strongly? And how could she compete with all of them? If James was just like some lord of the land, gathering females around him to display his virility and status, she wanted no part of it. But was that all that he was after? A primitive thrill that was no better than an animal's instincts? Or was he genuinely interested in her as a person?

A cold feeling of doubt attacked her as she watched him come striding out of the deer enclosure and lock the gate behind him. She felt herself stiffening warily, as if she were trying to erect some kind of invisible barrier between them. Better not to lose her head! It was one thing to admit to herself in private that she had these strange, aching longings for James Fraser, but it would be madness to let him guess what she felt.

Probably he had women falling for him all the time. If he knew the way her heart pounded at the mere sight of him he might find her ridiculous, or even pitiable, and that was more than she could bear. Worse still, he might decide to try and seduce her. Laura wasn't stupid. She knew she was attractive, and she had seen the gleam of interest in James's eyes, but if he simply used her and then discarded her the pleasure wouldn't be worth the pain that would follow. No. She must stick to her guns and be the kind of person she had always been. Cautious. Sensible. Aloof. That way she would be safe.

Fortunately James didn't seem to have any dangerous designs on her, at least for the moment. As he flipped the reins over his horse's head and swung himself adroitly into the saddle he gave her a brief, preoccupied smile.

'We'll go to the beach now,' he promised.

The strange motion of the horse was becoming a bit more familiar, so that Laura felt brave enough to stop staring apprehensively at the ground and actually raise her head and look around her. The experience was exhilarating. They were riding on a narrow track which led through bushland with glimpses of the sea on one side and the tranquil green fields on the other. Although there were still beads of moisture clinging like diamonds to the fence wires, the cloudless blue sky overhead and the bright sunshine gave promise of a fine day to come.

Laura drew in deep breaths of the fresh, eucalypt-scented air and felt as if all the tensions of her old life were draining away.

'This is so different from Sydney!' she exclaimed. 'I know we have a beautiful harbour and wonderful beaches there, but sometimes the traffic noise and the petrol fumes are unbearable. This is unbelievably peaceful.'

James glanced over his shoulder at her and smiled with a touch of bitterness.

'I'm glad you like it. Some women detest it.'

There was so much pent-up feeling in his voice that Laura wondered uneasily whether he was referring to his ex-wife. Since she didn't know him well enough to ask, and wasn't the inquisitive type anyway, there seemed little she could say. All the same, she gazed thoughtfully at his broad, upright back as they continued their way along the track.

Why had his wife left him? Hadn't Wendy said something about it, implying that it hadn't been James's fault? 'His wife Paula treated him pretty badly...' Hadn't that been it? But what had she done? Suddenly Laura felt a passionate urge to know, to reach out to James, to ask him, but she had the feeling that she would only meet with a sarcastic rebuff if she did.

Shaking her head, she turned her attention back to her surroundings and was rewarded by the sight of a wattle tree in full bloom, with its golden cascades of flowers hanging in profusion over the track and scenting the air around them with a sweet, pervasive fragrance. What did it matter anyway? The best thing she could do was simply to enjoy the present and forget about everything else.

'There's the beach,' said James, gesturing up ahead to the point where the track disappeared over a ridge. 'Can you hear the surf?'

Laura listened and was rewarded by the sound of thundering waves.

'Yes, I can.'

'Well, we'll go down to the firm sand near the water's edge and you can try trotting. That's always a bit tricky the first time.'

I bet I'll master it, thought Laura to herself. She was rather pleased with the way she was getting used to the horse's gait, and was in an optimistic mood that made her feel ready to conquer the world. As they reached the water's edge, and the white foam washed in eddies around the horses' hooves, she listened impatiently to James's instructions.

'Try and go with the motion of the horse. It's called rising to the trot. If you stand up in the stirrups, you might find it easier. Watch what I'm doing and imitate it.'

He kicked the gelding's flanks and they moved off together in a precise, fluid motion that looked perfectly easy to Laura until without warning her mare took off as well. Suddenly Laura felt herself being jolted up and down like a sack of potatoes while simultaneously being pounded violently in the most uncomfortable places. With a startled shriek she lost one of her stirrups, and in trying to slip her foot back into it lost her hold on the reins as well.

'Stop! Stop!' she begged, clutching at the horse's mane and watching the sand jolt blurrily beneath her. Would it hurt much if she fell off? 'S-t-o-p, you awful beast!'

A moment later James had wheeled round and was cantering back to rescue her. In a few effortless movements, he halted the mare, restored the reins to Laura, found her dangling stirrup and thrust her foot into it. There was no mistaking the gleam of amusement in his eyes.

'I'm hopeless, aren't I?' she wailed in embarrassment.

For an instant his hand lingered on her ankle, then he straightened up in the saddle and gave her a look that made her feel more flustered than ever.

'No, you're infuriating and hard to fathom,' he said in measured tones. 'But I wouldn't say you were hopeless.'

Laura had little time to wonder about his meaning during the next half-hour as James worked ruthlessly on her riding skills. By the end of that time she had experienced every emotion from utter frustration to sheer, gibbering terror, but she had also had two or three exhilarating tastes of success, when the tricky rhythm had come to her by magic, only to be lost again.

'All right,' said James at last. 'I think you've earned a cup of coffee.'

Her face fell.

'Do we have to stop now? I'm just starting to get the hang of it and I don't want to go back to the house yet.'

'If you don't stop now, you won't be able to walk tomorrow,' he warned. 'But we needn't go back to the house just yet if you don't want to. There's a nice little spot about half a mile away where I can build a fire and make some coffee. From now on we'll just walk the horses.'

Glowing with pride and the invigorating effects of the sea breeze, Laura turned her horse obediently in pursuit of James. This time they did not go back the way they had come, but instead took a dirt road which led off towards a headland. It was flanked by an avenue of massive pine trees whose huge branches met overhead, making the space beneath them as hushed and shadowy as the interior of a cathedral. Laura craned her neck back to look at them and sniffed appreciatively at the pine-scented air.

'What beautiful trees!' she exclaimed. 'They look as if they've been here for centuries.'

'That's just about right. My great-great-great-grandfather planted them in 1837.'

'You mean your tie with the land goes back that far? That's a tremendous privilege.'

'I suppose so,' he said tersely. 'There are also times when it's a tremendous burden.'

He didn't explain what he meant, and she didn't ask him, but once again she had the uncomfortable suspicion that he was talking about his ex-wife. Before long the road came to an end in a semi-circle of gravel in front of an old-fashioned octagonal summer house, complete with a slate roof, iron lace trim and a weathercock on the summit. Laura stared at it in delight.

'Isn't it beautiful? Does that date back to 1837 too?'

'The original building does, but it's been repaired so many times there can't be much of that left. We often have barbecues here in the summer. There's plenty of firewood and the creek's handy for running water.'

He jerked his head in the direction of a clump of trees behind the summer house and Laura caught a glimpse of clear sparkling water rushing over a rocky bed. While she was still gazing at it, entranced, he dismounted and walked across to the summer house.

Laura attempted to follow, but as she swung her right leg over the horse's back and scrambled to the ground something strange happened.

'Whoa!' she exclaimed. 'My legs have just turned to rubber.'

'Do you want me to carry you?' James offered, turning back to look at her with a sardonic smile.

Did she? In the world of her fantasies the offer would have been irresistible. But here, surrounded by the reality of being alone with him in the bush, it was entirely too disturbing for Laura's comfort. She shook her head.

'No, thanks,' she said with a grimace. 'I'll just crawl, I think. Have you got somewhere quiet where I can lie down and die?'

'Try the picnic table next to the barbecue,' suggested James. 'I'll just tie up the horses, then make a fire and some coffee. Perhaps that will revive you.'

Every bone in Laura's body ached as if it had been broken, and her muscles seemed to have been wrenched permanently out of shape, but it was pleasant to sit at the wooden table and watch James as he got the fire going. First he brought some small sticks and newspapers from inside the summer house and made a pyramid of wood and crumpled paper. When that was blazing brightly with orange flames, he started to add larger pieces of dry wood from a stack sheltered by the brick overhang of the barbecue. Then he brought out an old iron kettle from the summer house, filled it from the creek and set it to boil on the grid. Last of all he produced mugs from the summer house, and a jar of coffee and a screw-top bottle of milk from his saddle-bag.

'You're very efficient,' said Laura admiringly.

'My mother taught me to be at an early age.'

'Is she still alive?'

'Yes.'

'I didn't meet her at the wedding.'

'She didn't come. Sam's father Adrian is only my half-brother from my father's first marriage, so my mother isn't actually related to Sam at all. When my father died, she moved back to America, which is where she originally came from. These days she doesn't move out of Pennsylvania much. In fact, I don't think she even moves out of the local shopping mall. There was an unconfirmed sighting in Hawaii in December last year, when

Wendy swears she saw her at a linen sale in a big department store, but I think it was just a delusion.'

Laura smiled.

'How did she meet your father? Did their eyes meet across a crowded check-out counter?'

James shook his head.

'No. She wasn't a shopaholic thirty-eight years ago. He met her on a Caribbean cruise not long after his first wife died. Heaven knows what she saw in him. He was twenty years older than her and a widower with a child into the bargain. Still, I've got to admit that he could be charming if you didn't know him well.'

'Ouch,' winced Laura. 'That sounds as if you didn't like him much.'

James tossed another chunk of wood on the fire and scowled thoughtfully.

'We didn't really get along,' he admitted.

'What went wrong?'

'Right from the start he was the kind of man that had to be in control of everything, and nobody could do things as well as he could, so he was always incredibly critical. Wendy just thumbed her nose at him, but for some stupid reason I always wanted to please him. Then when I was nineteen we had a massive quarrel.'

'What about?'

Suddenly James's eyes looked veiled and opaque. He shrugged his shoulders.

'Oh, just a difference of opinion on how I should live my life. He wanted me to go to Harvard to do a business degree, and I didn't want to go. So I didn't. I left home instead and became a deckhand on a tuna boat.'

A series of expressions flitted across his face as he spoke, like shadows chasing across a landscape. Laura had the impression that there was a lot more that he wasn't telling her, but she didn't feel brave enough to ask him outright for more detail. Instead she approached the subject obliquely.

'Did you ever patch it up?'

'After a fashion, we did. So much so that I moved back to Tasmania and took over managing this property when he was in his last illness.'

'Were you living somewhere else by then?' she asked in surprise.

Somehow James seemed to belong so completely on this unspoilt island that she could not imagine him anywhere else.

'Yes, I was in California,' he said. 'I'd started a transport company there and was doing very well.'

He turned away to deal with the coffee and the conversation lapsed. But later, when they were sipping from their fragrant, steaming mugs, Laura raised the topic again.

'Were you sorry to leave California?'

James sighed.

'Yes and no. I liked the excitement of the place, and the thrill of power and achievement that came from being successful there, but other aspects of life in the fast lane didn't appeal to me. In the end I had to make a choice about what was most important. My father had had a stroke and was past managing the farm, and my mother didn't have the skills to run it. He threatened to sell the place if I didn't take over. I wasn't sure what I was going to do, but I came home to visit him, expecting that he'd be changed by his illness and treat me like the long-lost beloved son.'

'And did he?'

James gave a harsh growl of laughter.

'No, he most certainly did not! He was the same cantankerous old cuss as ever. Full of criticism about everything I'd done since I'd seen him last. I was so desperate to get away from him before I punched him in the nose that I came out here for a ride. That was a mistake.'

'Why?'

'Because once I saw this avenue of pine trees and the little summer house at the end, I knew I could never give it up to anybody else. I knew I belonged here.'

She nodded thoughtfully. If she had known him better she would have reached out and gripped his hand.

'Do you ever go back to California?'

'Yes, two or three times a year. I still have business interests there. I travel to Europe and South East Asia too, but this is my home.'

'Was your father grateful when you gave up everything to come back here?' she asked.

'If he was, he didn't show it. To his dying day he picked and carped about everything I did. But the funny thing is, he left everything in his will to me, which meant a lot to me. Not because of the money—I've made ten times as much as that myself—but because of the hidden message. I felt he was telling me that he could trust me to handle everything he owned and do the right thing by everyone. Yes, I suppose you could say we patched it up.'

'That's a really sad story,' murmured Laura.

'No, it isn't! It's a very common story. People choose what they want to do and live with the consequences. That's what I did and I've got no complaints. Now, come on, it's time we were heading back.'

Ten minutes later they were moving sedately back along the beach when they saw another horse cantering towards them. As it drew closer Laura noticed that the rider wore jodhpurs, polished boots, a hacking jacket and a neat velvet riding cap. She sat gracefully upright in the saddle and moved as if she and the horse were a single entity. Raising her riding crop in greeting, she called to them as she came splashing through the shallows towards them.

'Hello, James! I've got something important I want to discuss with you.'

James's features took on a keen, interested expression, and he urged his horse forward.

'What is it, Sue?' he asked.

CHAPTER FIVE

Sue let her chestnut horse dance skittishly around in the foam for a moment before she answered. Laura had the unworthy suspicion that she only did this so that she could display her slim legs and the skill with which she brought the snorting animal under control. All her own good humour drained away as she watched the other woman lean forward and address James confidingly, without even acknowledging her presence.

'I've got a copy of the shopping centre plan and it's just as bad as we feared. They want to put it smack bang in the middle of the village and tear down six beautiful old houses to do it. Not only that, but that avenue of hundred-and-fifty-year-old oak trees would have to go.'

James included Laura in the conversation by means of an apologetic glance.

'You remember Sue from the wedding, don't you? She's been spearheading a campaign against architectural vandalism in the village. A development company is hoping to put in a supermarket complex which will wreck a really beautiful area if it's allowed to go ahead. Not that I'm against development, but that's definitely the wrong site for it. Can I come and look at the plans, Sue?'

'Of course. The sooner the better.'

'We'll come now, if you like,' offered James. 'We can put the horses in your back paddock and Laura can sit and put her feet up while we sort this out.'

Sue's green eyes narrowed.

'Oh, I don't think Laura would be interested,' she said swiftly. 'It's only a local matter, after all. Why don't you come back this evening and see them properly? I'm sure Laura wouldn't mind staying at your house and watching a video or something.'

'Well—' began Laura.

'No, it's better to get it done now,' cut in James. 'I want to see my lawyers in Hobart tomorrow, and there's no point doing that until I've had a good look at the plans. Besides, I'm sure Laura would like to see your house.'

Sue's smile was tight-lipped.

'All right,' she agreed ungraciously.

Sue's house proved to be one of the old sandstone buildings in a quiet street only a short distance from the proposed development, with an acre of lush green gardens, a paddock and stone stables behind it. When they had tied up the horses, Sue led them into a pine-lined kitchen, where sunlight splashed in through tall windows divided into numerous tiny panes of glass. Waving them towards a table and chairs of Huon pine, she switched on the electric jug and lifted down an old-fashioned tin.

'You will have some coffee, won't you?'

'We've already had some, but I'd be glad of another cup,' said James. 'What about you, Laura?'

'Yes, please.'

'Oh, dear,' cried Sue, lifting the lid of the tin and pulling a comical face. 'It looks as though I'm out of your Arabica, James. I'll have to give you Kenyan instead. But we have got some of those hazelnut wafers you like. Try one, Laura, they're nine million calories a bite, but utterly yummy. Fortunately I don't have to worry about my figure, since I'm naturally slim.'

She accompanied this statement with a smug sidelong glance at Laura's thighs that made her feel like the Michelin tyre man. Laura felt an unexpected flare of annoyance, and hit back without pausing to think.

'Isn't it funny,' she murmured as Sue set the plate of biscuits on the table, 'how the concept of the ideal shape of a woman has changed so much? During most of history, thin women were considered freaks and were thought very unattractive. As a matter of fact, I think most men still secretly believe that. You're lucky you were born when you were, Sue.'

The other girl forced a laugh, but the tension in the air was as oppressive as if a thunderstorm were brewing. James cleared his throat diplomatically.

'What about the plans?' he reminded Sue.

'Oh, yes,' she said, wiping her hands on her jodhpurs and casting Laura a poisonous glance. 'I've left them in my bedroom. I'll go and get them.' She returned a moment later with a blueprint in one hand and a large striped blue T-shirt in the other. 'By the way, is this yours?'

James peered at it and gave a surprised laugh.

'Yes, I think it is. Thanks very much. I must have left it here last time I came.'

'You ought to be careful where you take your clothes off, darling,' said Sue in a sultry voice.

James opened his mouth as if to speak, and evidently thought better of it. Spreading out the plans, he anchored them with some crockery and began scowling thoughtfully at them.

Laura watched them both with a miserable feeling of resentment as all her old distrust of Sam's uncle came flooding back. She hated the smug way that Sue was hovering over the coffee percolator and occasionally casting proprietorial glances at James, she hated the way he was looking through the plans with total absorption, as if nothing was wrong, and most of all she hated herself for being upset by it.

When the coffee was finally made, James plunged into a complicated discussion with Sue about the supermarket development and Laura was left feeling that she was invisible, inaudible and totally unimportant. She fumed in silence until he suddenly turned and smiled at her.

'Sorry, Laura,' he exclaimed. 'We've no manners at all. Let's talk about something else. Did I tell you Sam phoned last night to say they've reached Singapore safely and are going on to Europe next week for the rest of their honeymoon?'

'Oh, really?' said Laura frostily. 'How interesting.'

Sue made no attempt to hide her amusement at Laura's discomfiture and she soon made another bid to flaunt her involvement with James. Laying her hand on his arm, she smiled winningly at him.

'Are you going to take me to the Rotary Ball next month?' she demanded.

James frowned.

'Won't Jack be home by then?'

'The only place I want to see Jack again is in a divorce court!' she retorted bitterly.

'Sue!' James's voice was stern. 'That's something we should discuss in private, and I'll be happy to do so, but this is neither the time nor the place for it.'

'Sorry.' Sue's face suddenly looked like a frozen mask, and she gripped James's arm so tightly that her knuckles stood out white against her skin, making Laura feel almost sorry for her. Darting Laura a brief, resentful glance, she spoke again in a choking voice. 'Will you come back later so we can talk about it?'

James's arm stiffened, as if he wanted to pull away from her, but he nodded reluctantly.

'All right.'

'Thank you,' said Sue fervently.

As they were leaving she said goodbye grudgingly to Laura, but suddenly reached on her tiptoes and kissed James on the cheek. His exasperated look softened and he put one arm around her and hugged her. Sue's eyes glowed.

'We'll discuss the supermarket plans too, when you come back tonight,' she promised. 'We'll really put our heads together.'

It looks to me as if she's hoping they'll put more than just their heads together, thought Laura sourly as she followed James out to the place where the horses were tethered. What on earth is going on here? It doesn't take a towering genius to see that Sue's head over heels in love with James and that she's hoping to stay with him once her divorce comes through, but then, what does he want?

It looks as though he's having an affair with her, but why does he lead her on one minute and slam the door in her face the next? Has he been having an affair with her and now he's horrified to find that she took it more seriously than he did? Did he only want a meaningless sexual romp with her that wouldn't lead anywhere? Laura's lips curled contemptuously. It looked to her as if James was searching for an escape route from Sue's demands. Well, it would be interesting to see whether he accepted her invitation and went back that evening.

Rather to Laura's surprise, he did.

'I'll only be gone for an hour or so,' he said as he shrugged himself into his sheepskin jacket. 'Are you sure this doesn't bother you?'

'It's nothing to do with me,' said Laura coldly. 'Stay away as long as you like.'

It was more than two and a half hours before he returned, and when he entered the living room she spotted immediately that his dark hair was damp and clinging to his neck, as if he had just come out of the shower. She was unprepared for the pang of jealousy and pain that went through her at this observation.

'Look, I've been thinking,' she burst out. 'I don't know that it's such a good idea for me to stay here. I'd rather go home.'

He gave her a long, level stare and pursed his lips thoughtfully.

'Does this decision have anything to do with Sue and me?' he challenged.

'No,' she retorted, tossing her head.

'Good. Because my friendship with Sue has absolutely nothing to do with what's happening between you and me.'

'There's nothing happening between you and me,' she said hastily.

'You're wrong,' he murmured. 'A lot is happening.'

His voice was husky, caressing, unbearably sensual so that it sent little trickles of excitement running down her spine. He didn't touch her, which was just as well. In the midst of her torment, that invasion of her personal space would have been far too threatening to endure. With a little shock of disbelief, she realised that she would probably haul off and slap his face if he so much as laid a finger on her. What was happening to her?

She had never imagined she could experience such violent emotions. How could the smoky quality of his voice, the narrowed appraisal of his golden eyes have such a profoundly unsettling effect on her? And how could she go on feeling so dangerously attracted to him now that she was almost convinced he was sleeping with Sue Rigby? She should never have trusted him! When he stepped forward a pace, she flinched and moved away.

'I don't think I've ever been so attracted to any woman in my life as I am to you,' he continued thoughtfully.

Panic made her voice unnaturally sharp.

'Am I supposed to be flattered by that?'

'There's no need to be sarcastic,' he observed with a lazy tilt of his eyebrows. 'No, you're not supposed to be flattered, but it would help if you were honest about it. Why can't you just admit that you feel the same violent current of attraction as I do?'

'B-because I don't!' stammered Laura.

James took another step forward, so that he was looming over her, close enough to see the rapid, irregular rise and fall of her breathing.

'Liar,' he murmured. 'All the evidence says that you do. Your erratic heartbeat, your shallow breathing, the flush around your cheeks and neck.'

An even more burning wave of crimson rushed into Laura's face and she dropped her eyes.

'That could just mean that I'm agitated because you're making unwanted advances to me.'

He shook his head and put his hands ostentatiously on his hips, as if to prove that he had no intention of touching her.

'I'm not making any advances to you.'

'Yes, you are!' she cried, stung by the unfairness of the statement. 'You're... you're looking at me!'

'And that's enough to set you on fire?' he marvelled. 'Well, I suppose that's fair enough, because it's exactly the same for me. All I have to do is look at you and I begin burning with need for you.'

Laura's head swam as she felt a dizzy rush of mingled exhilaration and outrage.

'I don't believe you!'

'It's the truth.'

'I don't want to hear it!' she exclaimed in a suffocated voice, pressing her cool palms against her hot face. 'All I want to do is go home!'

'Why?' he demanded mockingly. 'Are you too embarrassed to face the truth? Well, don't be, Laura! There's no need for you to be ashamed of wanting me.'

'I'm not ashamed... Anyway, I don't... Oh, leave me alone!' she exclaimed incoherently.

His voice was cool, precise, amused—in maddening contrast to hers.

'I think the way you're behaving makes it clear enough what your feelings are, don't you?' he said, laying one hand lightly on her shoulder.

'Let me go!' she breathed, twisting away.

'What are you frightened of?'

'I'm not frightened of anything!'

'Then why do you deny what's happening between us?'

She backed away from him again, and found the hard surface of the wall was blocking her escape. Unable to flee any further, she was forced to stop and confront him. And that taunting gleam in his eyes also forced her to confront what was happening inside her.

'I'm not denying anything. All right, I admit that you're quite...er...physically, well... Oh, stop smirking at me like that! All right, you're sexually attractive!

There, I've said it! Satisfied? But maybe I just don't want to be used and then thrown away.'

'Whatever gave you the idea that I'd do that?' he drawled.

'Wendy gave me the idea that you would!' shouted Laura. 'She told me that you lead women on and then discard them.'

James didn't deny the charge. He simply shrugged, as if it were of no importance. The coolness with which he ignored the accusation gave her the panicky feeling that he was playing some kind of cruel game with her. While she blundered around in a highly charged emotional state he seemed to be no more than a detached observer, watching her struggles with amusement. The thought infuriated her.

'You don't get involved with women, do you?' she cried passionately. 'Not really involved? Oh, I don't doubt that you wine them and dine them and take them to bed, but you don't really care, do you? You never lay yourself open to pain and you don't give anything of yourself, do you?'

He was silent for a moment, watching her intently with an unfathomable expression in his golden eyes. Wave after wave of longing and anger and despair broke over her as she tried to match him stare for stare. But it was useless. He was as cool and impassive as a granite cliff-face, while she felt as turbulent as a stormy sea. To her annoyance she discovered that her hands were shaking. She bit her lip, willing herself not to lapse into the ultimate humiliation of tears. Then James spoke.

'Maybe this time it will turn out differently,' he said in an odd, abrupt voice.

Laura made a rude noise.

'Oh, yes! And maybe this time I'll turn out to be Madonna in disguise.'

Her scathing joke broke the tension. James's face contorted in a vain attempt to hold back laughter and suddenly their eyes met. A vivid image of Laura in black leather and a cone-shaped bra seemed to hover in the air between them. Then James's laughter exploded.

'Now, that would be worth seeing,' he said appreciatively.

She was almost relieved by the sudden lightening of the mood, which gave her a chance to bring her unruly emotions under control. Even when his mirth subsided, and he reached out and touched her hair, she did no more than stiffen warily.

'What exactly are you frightened of?' he asked. 'Do you think I'm going to rape you?'

'Of course not,' she retorted. 'I don't believe your approach would be that crude. Anyway, there are laws against that sort of thing.'

Twining her hair around his finger, he looked down at her and deliberately let his voice deepen and thicken even further, as if he were a stage villain in a Victorian melodrama. His eyes flickered maniacally.

'Or do you think I'm going to use my vile, irresistible charm to lure you into my bed against your will?' he taunted.

Actually, that was exactly what Laura did fear, but she certainly didn't want to make herself ridiculous by admitting it.

'I'm not as stupid as that!'

'Then where's the danger?' asked James, reverting to his normal voice. Even that had a hoarse, elusive quality that Laura found unbearably provocative. 'Forewarned is forearmed, isn't it? If I give you my word that I won't use any unfair tactics to coerce or persuade you, what's the problem? It seems to me the only remaining risk is in your own feelings, and those are under your control, not mine.'

No, they're not, thought Laura despairingly. They haven't been under my control from the moment I met you. Yet she did not say this aloud.

'That's all very well,' she replied coolly. 'But what exactly are you asking me to do?'

He drew the long, dark silky strand of her hair across his knuckles and brushed it across his lips.

'Just stay on and see what develops,' he urged. 'Didn't you give me an impassioned speech about the importance of taking risks in relationships the first time you were here? Or were you just being Bea, and not yourself on that occasion?'

'I don't know who I was being!' burst out Laura. 'Ever since I first undertook that ridiculous masquerade, I've been acting in ways that are totally out of character for me. I feel as if I don't know who I am any more.'

'Then stay and find out. It's a healthy thing, Laura. You're finally breaking out of the strait-jacket that your duty has kept you imprisoned in for years. I know that must be frightening for you, but let it happen. Take the risk of exploring your desire for me.'

Interesting, his choice of word, thought Laura. Not love, not yearning for intimacy, but desire.

'I wish I knew what you meant by that,' she said bitterly.

James released his hold on her hair and spread his arms wide in an expansive gesture.

'It's very simple,' he explained. 'I just want us to get to know each other.'

'How can I be sure you won't take advantage of me?'

'You'll have to trust me. I won't insult your intelligence by swearing an oath that there's nothing going on between Sue Rigby and me—' I wish you would! thought Laura miserably '—but I will promise you this. I won't try to rush things with you. I won't do anything that you don't agree to and want just as passionately as I do.'

Considering the dreams she had been having about James ever since she'd first met him, that didn't seem to be much of a restriction. Laura sighed, pressed her fingers to her aching temples and stared in perplexity at the floor.

'That's a great comfort,' she muttered sceptically.

She could feel the smile on James's face as he lowered his head to hers and nuzzled her hair.

'Well?' he coaxed. 'What's it going to be? Are you going to be brave and stay on? Or are you going to run away because you don't have the courage to take a chance on yourself?'

She raised her head and looked him directly in the eye.

'What a gift you have for expressing yourself,' she observed. 'I think you're wasted as a farmer. Why didn't you go into high-pressure marketing?'

'There are too many heartless, sceptical women among the consumers,' he replied lightly. Then his voice changed and a new note of earnestness entered it. 'Well, Laura? What's it to be? This time there's no pressure, no smart sales talk. Just a simple, honest statement. I want you to stay. Will you?'

She was unexpectedly touched by the sincerity in his voice and by the directness of his gaze. Her misgivings dissolved and she let out her breath in a long sigh.

'All right, James. I'll stay.'

*   *   *

James was already in the kitchen reading a financial newspaper when Laura came down to breakfast the following morning. He glanced up, pushed the coffee-pot and the plate of warm blueberry muffins towards her and then looked down again as if he hadn't really seen her. Laura smothered a grin as he began punching in numbers on a pocket calculator and muttering to himself.

On the rare occasions when Bea had surfaced before eleven o'clock in the morning, they had always quarrelled over Laura's antisocial habit of remaining glued to the financial news throughout breakfast. It was rather nice to meet a fellow delinquent at last. Laura stifled a giggle.

'What are you laughing at?' demanded James suspiciously, raising his head.

'You,' she replied, helping herself to coffee and muffins. 'I thought I was the only one who muttered about put and call options throughout breakfast.'

'Hmm,' grunted James, setting down the newspaper. 'I'm getting too used to living on my own, that's the trouble. Tell me, Laura, how long are you able to stay here?'

She blinked, taken aback by the question.

'How long do you want me to stay?' she asked.

His eyes gleamed.

'As long as possible.'

'You might be sorry you said that. Technically speaking, I'm entitled to another seven weeks' leave from my job, since I didn't take any holidays last year.'

'Good,' he said with satisfaction, folding the newspaper and tossing it aside onto a kitchen cupboard. 'In that case, I hope you'll stay for seven weeks.'

Excitement sang in her veins. Wasn't it a promising sign if he wanted her to be his guest for so long? On the other hand, she didn't want to become a burden to him.

'Are you sure?'

'Yes,' he said simply. 'Now, do you want to drive down to Hobart today and shop for some clothes?'

His tone was as matter-of-fact as if they were a husband and wife discussing their plans for the day. Laura couldn't help feeling warmed by the intimacy of it, but she was also perplexed. In her view, James's insistence that she should stay for so long implied that something serious was happening between them. And yet he seemed to regard it as merely one more detail to be approved before moving on to the next item. Or was it only a trivial issue to him anyway? Did he invite women to stay for two months at a time so often that he lost count of them all?

A perplexed frown knitted her brows, and then she realised that he was still gazing keenly at her, waiting for an answer to his question.

'What? Oh, sorry. Yes, I do want to go shopping today, please. I must get some things to wear.'

'I have credit accounts at several big department stores. I'd be happy to—'

'No!' Accepting his hospitality was one thing, letting him buy her clothes was entirely another matter. The mere thought gave her an uncomfortable feeling in the pit of her stomach, as if she were surrendering her integrity. Then he saw his look of mild surprise at the fierceness of her tone and wondered if she was overreacting. Her voice emerged, half-defiant, half-uncertain, when she spoke again. 'I couldn't possibly allow you to do that! It wouldn't be proper.'

'Proper!' He gave a snort of amusement and reached forward to ruffle her hair. 'You're a gem, Laura. Circa 1915, but a gem nevertheless. Don't ever change, will you?'

It annoyed her to see him laughing at her, even if the laughter was indulgent. Why did everyone think she was Miss Prissy? Deep down, she knew she wasn't like that at all. Well, one of these days she would break out and surprise them all! She gazed at him coldly.

'Oh, come on!' he coaxed. 'Don't be offended. I like the kind of person you are, Laura. Now, finish your breakfast, get dressed and let's get moving. It's a three-hour journey and I've got some business to transact at the woollen mill before noon. After that I suggest we go to the casino for lunch, then split up for a few hours. You can go shopping while I see my solicitors about the challenge to the shopping complex. Then we'll meet again for tea and drive back. How does that sound?'

'All right,' agreed Laura grudgingly.

As she trailed upstairs she gritted her teeth and wondered yet again about the wisdom of the whole enterprise. Sometimes she liked James, really liked him a lot. When he'd been teaching her to ride, for instance, he had been really kind and patient. And when he'd talked about giving up his own business in order to take over the firm for his cantankerous old father, she had felt a genuine rush of sympathy for him. But there were other occasions when she wanted to hit him. Like now, for instance.

If his sister was right and he was nothing but a playboy, what was she, Laura Madison, doing with him? She must be insane! And now she faced a three-hour drive during which he would probably bait her about her quaint scruples on taking money from men. Nice going, Laura, she told herself. Looks as if you've organised a great holiday.

Rather to her surprise, James didn't bait her during the trip to Hobart. In fact, he seemed to go out of his way to be pleasant without probing any uncomfortable subjects. He talked about everything under the sun. Favourite foods, favourite films, the weather, music, business, politics, childhood ambitions and pet hates. And he showed an uncanny knack for drawing out her opinions too.

By the time the brick chimneys of the woollen mill rose into view against the blue backdrop of the Derwent estuary, Laura felt she had known James all her life. Not that she necessarily liked everything she had discovered about him—far from it! Although he was undoubtedly intelligent, forceful and a stimulating companion, he could also be downright pig-headed on a number of issues. All the same, she couldn't deny that her ruffled feathers were soothed and that she was beginning to find him more complex and intriguing than she had ever guessed.

After a brief tour of the woollen mill, James took her to lunch in the revolving restaurant at the casino. By now Laura was beginning to wilt from the combined effects of a long drive and an hour of industrial detail, but her spirits revived at the sight of the view. When a smiling waiter showed them to their seats at a table by the window, she caught her breath in amazement.

'What an incredible panorama! You must be able to see for fifty miles, and there's so much variety. The mountain, the city, the sea, and ... are those offshore islands?'

'Peninsulas, more likely, although it's hard to tell. Anyway, if we eat at exactly the right pace, the restaurant should do one full circuit of the tower so that you can see everything before you leave. Now, would you like something to drink?'

'Yes, a gin and tonic, please.'

Laura sat down in the comfortable upholstered chair, enjoying the opulence of the starched tablecloth, the flowers, the silver, the attractive china. From time to time she had taken clients of the firm out to expense account lunches in equally good restaurants in Sydney, but in her own private life she had always been thrifty. At first she hadn't had much money to splash around and later she had been saving for a home of her own. Even now it gave her a thrill to be eating out in a place like this, although James seemed as relaxed and casual as if it were his natural environment.

After a reviving drink they studied the menu and Laura opted for smoked salmon followed by fillet steak with salad, while James chose a lobster bisque and an Italian veal dish with fried potatoes. After ordering, they sat back and smiled at each other while the waiter poured white wine for them.

'Cheers,' said James.

'Cheers,' echoed Laura.

As she lifted her glass she accidentally dislodged a small white flower from the glass vase between them. It fell out on the tablecloth and James picked it up and put it back in the water.

'There were hundreds of these things in the paddock next to the deer enclosure a week or two ago,' he remarked. 'Snowdrops, aren't they?'

'Snowflakes,' Laura corrected. 'You can tell by the little green dots on the petals.'

James's eyes widened.

'I thought Bea was the one who'd studied horticulture, not you.'

Laura twinkled at him.

'Well, she probably only did it because I pushed her
into it,' she admitted. 'I've always loved growing things.
My biggest ambition in life is to have a garden.'

'Don't you have one at the moment?'

She shook her head.

'No. I wanted to buy a home of my own, but with
Sydney prices as they are, the best I could afford was a
two-bedroom flat.'

James sipped his wine and rolled it round reflectively
on his tongue before he spoke.

'You told me once that you'd like to go to Queensland
and visit the rainforests. Was that your ambition or
Bea's?'

'Mine,' said Laura. 'Most of what I told you was really
about me, although it's very odd, really. Somehow, when
I was talking to you, I kept discovering things about
myself that I never knew before. I didn't even know until
I said it that I wanted to go to Queensland.'

'Then do it!' urged James. 'I think it's a mistake to
have passionate longings for experience and do nothing
about it.'

'You said you wanted to go to Queensland too, and
ride horses and laze about on the beach,' she reminded
him. 'Are you going to do that?'

'Perhaps we should join forces and do it together,' he
said half to himself. 'Go beachcombing and visit the
national parks. Combine our interests.'

Laura suffered such a shock at these words that she
choked on her wine and was seized by a coughing fit.
By the time her eyes had stopped streaming the waiter
had arrived with the smoked salmon and lobster bisque

and James was busy ordering her a glass of water. She felt too embarrassed to try and re-open the subject, particularly since her voice was temporarily reduced to a croak, but she pondered James's words as she cautiously began to eat her smoked salmon. This was the first time he had ever suggested that their relationship might have any future beyond the immediate one, but did he mean it? Or was it merely idle conversation? She watched him covertly from under her eyelashes, trying to read his face.

'Better now?' he asked.

She nodded and took another sip of water.

'Yes. Sorry about that.'

'That's all right. How's the smoked salmon?'

'Excellent, thank you.'

The conversation turned to food, and she was almost relieved when they spent the remainder of the meal in the same kind of light-hearted, fluent discussion that had occupied their journey that morning. Only when James called for the bill did a warning note sound in her thoughts.

'I'd better be off,' he said, looking at his watch. 'I promised Sue I'd see my solicitors about this shopping complex and they're expecting me at two-thirty. Are you ready to go?'

'Yes, of course,' she agreed, but she felt as if a chill, damp blanket had descended on her spirits at the mention of Sue Rigby's name. Were she and James really only allies in the fight against the developers, or was there more to it than that?

They parted company in the centre of the city and James pointed out the central shopping district to her.

'You can't go wrong,' he advised. 'Basically everything's located in the one city block, so buy whatever you can in two hours and meet me at the Sheraton at four-thirty. We'll have a quick cup of tea before we drive home.'

Laura enjoyed her shopping. Normally she bought well-cut, conservative clothes that would be suitable for the office, but this time some experimental demon seemed to have taken possession of her. At first she chose the kind of classic, understated clothes she had always favoured—mix and match corduroy trousers, a couple of skirts, three blouses, a cardigan and a sweater—but in the last half-hour she went berserk. Not only did she buy some extremely sexy black lace lingerie, but she chose a flamboyant scarlet dress and a scarlet, gold and black handbag which cost more than her round trip airline ticket to Sydney had done.

'Put my old clothes in the bag, please,' she told the sales assistant. 'I'm going to wear this dress.'

She had her reward when she walked into the atrium of the Sheraton Hotel and found James lounging in a chair against the huge windows that framed a view of the harbour. He blinked, rose to his feet and came forward to meet her with the stunned, admiring expression that Laura was accustomed to seeing when men met Beatrice for the first time.

'You look ravishing,' he said, holding her at arm's length and then kissing her on the cheek. 'What have you done to yourself?'

She smiled and sank into a chair, noticing with a mixture of embarrassment and delight that several other male heads were turning discreetly towards her.

'Oh, nothing,' she said. 'Just a few new clothes.'

'Well, they're the right sort of clothes,' said James warmly. 'You know, you leave your sister for dead, Laura. Poor kid, she's so skinny and gawky—even at the wedding you outclassed her. And now you look absolutely stunning.'

Laura gave a smothered gulp of laughter.

'But she's the beautiful one,' she protested.

'Not to me,' said James, his eyes glinting as they rested on her. Then he added in a voice so low she could scarcely catch his words, 'You know, I'm very glad you weren't marrying Sam.'

The waitress arrived at that moment to offer them some tea and the conversation moved to safer subjects. But later, as they were driving out of town, something else happened which made Laura wonder about James's plans for the future. They had just left the outskirts of the suburbs behind and were coming into more open country when Laura suddenly noticed a big advertising board outside a plant nursery.

'Oh, look!' she exclaimed. 'They've got lemon trees for sale. Do those really grow here? I would have thought it would be too cold for them.'

'No, they do very well, provided you buy the right variety and plant them in a sheltered spot,' said James. To her surprise, he slowed the car down. 'Do you want me to stop and buy one for you?'

'But I'll be here such a short time,' protested Laura. 'Lemon trees last for decades.'

The car glided to a halt outside the nursery. James switched off the ignition.

'Who knows how long you'll be here?' he said. 'A lot can happen in a short time.'

A lot did happen in a short time. Over the next few weeks Laura and James were inseparable, and her hopes began to grow that he was falling just as deeply in love with her as she was with him. Not that he tried to kiss her again, but the way his eyes lit up when she entered a room and the warmth with which they followed her left her in no doubt that he wanted to do so. She began to feel that he was deliberately going slowly in order to let her feel safe with him, although sometimes she suspected miserably that his strategy was exactly the opposite. Could he be going slowly in order to lull her suspicions and seduce her once her guard was down? Yet there seemed no real evidence for that.

As they shared the routine of work and play she began to feel as though he was not only the man she loved most in the world, but also her best friend. They went riding together, they planted the lemon tree and began landscaping the back garden together, they did the books for the farm together and they went to barbecues and car rallies and quiz nights with their neighbours. Laura began to feel as if she were settling into a whole new world, one where she could be very happy.

Yet there were two discordant notes which marred the harmony of her life. One was the realisation that she would very soon have to go back to Sydney to her job. The other was the fact that James still continued to see Sue Rigby. Matters came to a head when Sue invited them both to a barbecue in order to raise funds for the fight against the proposed shopping centre.

'I'm sorry,' said Laura as they sat in front of the living room fire the evening before the barbecue. 'I really don't want to go.'

'Why not?' demanded James in an exasperated voice.

'Well, to be brutally honest, I don't like her and I'm sure she doesn't like me, so it's only going to cause tension if I do go.'

'That's ridiculous! It will cause tension if you don't go and I've already said the same thing to her. I told her quite bluntly that she couldn't invite the whole village and not you.'

'There you are!' cried Laura. 'Obviously she didn't want me to come in the first place and she only invited me because you made her. Well, I'm not going where I'm not wanted.'

'I want you there!' snapped James. 'What's more, I'm insisting that you come.'

His arrogance took Laura's breath away.

'And I have to do exactly what you tell me, do I?' she retorted.

'Yes, if you want to put it that way. It's a question of loyalty. We've been invited as a couple and that's the way we'll go.'

As a couple. The words sent a stab of longing through Laura, followed by an equally acute pang of discontent. All the unsatisfactory aspects of their relationship rose and attacked her like a swarm of angry wasps.

'That's rubbish!' she burst out. 'We're not a couple. We're nothing like it! A couple is two people who have some kind of commitment to each other, who are emotionally involved with each other. Whereas we're just ships that pass in the night. I'm your house guest for a few weeks, you're my host, and before long we'll part and not even remember each other's faces.'

She gave a startled cry as James suddenly moved without warning. Uncoiling from his chair like a hunting cat, he crossed the open space between them, hauled her to her feet and crushed her in the most ruthless embrace she had ever experienced. Her blood seemed to throb through her veins like molten fire as he kissed her with a savagery that terrified and exhilarated her. Her legs felt too limp to support her as he engulfed her in his arms and plundered her mouth with a pent-up frenzy engendered by weeks of patient waiting.

'You're wrong,' he said hoarsely. 'We are a couple, and I'm going to prove it to you, Laura. In the most primitive way there is.'

CHAPTER SIX

SHE knew immediately what he intended and, after the first tremor of alarm, her heart soared at the realisation. When he gripped her hand and drew her towards the door she followed him gladly, although her legs seemed to have turned to water. All the familiar details of the house seemed touched with strangeness, as if her senses were unnaturally heightened by the importance of what they were about to do. James flung his arm around her shoulders as he urged her up the stairs and she leaned weakly against him, overtaken by joy and disbelief.

Even the polished cedar banisters sliding smoothly under her hand, the soft glow of the wall sconce on the landing and the creaking stair near the top seemed magically alive, as if they were witnesses to some tremendous event. He does love me, she thought. He loves me and wants me and now our union is going to be complete. And afterwards we'll get married and live in this beautiful house and have babies and... Oh, I'm so happy I could die. A couple. A real couple. At last.

The heavy cedar door of James's bedroom creaked open and he flicked a switch, which brought two softly glowing lamps on either side of his bed into shimmering life. Then the door creaked shut behind them and James drew her once more into that devouring embrace. His massive thighs were spread on either side of hers, trapping her against him, and his hands were moving rapidly over her shoulders and arms and breasts. Closing her eyes, she lifted her face to his, revelling in his open-mouthed kisses, in the hot, demanding pressure of his tongue against hers.

'I want you, Laura,' he said thickly. 'I want you so badly. Do you want me too?'

She shuddered as his hand moved over her breasts, stroking their satiny smoothness into hard, erect tips so that her entire body seemed to tingle and ache with need for him.

'Yes,' she gasped. 'Oh, yes. James—'

Her next words were lost in the low moan that overtook her as his hand slid down inside the waistband of her skirt, skimming the silken triangle of hair at the fork of her body and finding the most intimate part of her. She had never known such delirious pleasure could exist as the tingling excitement which maddened her now as his fingers moved subtly, caressingly against her.

'Touch me too,' he breathed, seizing her hand and guiding it.

Her heart was hammering so violently that she could hear the tumultuous thunder of her own pulse, but with inexpert fingers she cupped his hot, male hardness and began to stroke it. He uttered a low groan and suddenly wrenched at his clothes, tearing open the zip of his jeans so that she felt his rigid warmth pulsing in the palm of her hand. She glanced down in mingled alarm and excitement, wondering if she ought to tell him that she had never... wondering...

Then he kissed her so hotly that he seemed determined to suck the life out of her and she felt an aching warmth throb fiercely at her groin. Why tell him anything? He might stop, and that was the last thing she wanted now. Time enough for confidences when it was all over. With a faint whimper, she swayed against him, closing her eyes and feeling her breasts crush erotically against his powerful chest. When his hands moved expertly to peel off her skirt and tights, she felt only relief that the barrier was gone. Dizzily she sighed and nestled against him, wondering how and when she had kicked off her shoes. Then she closed her eyes and arched her back, offering herself to him provocatively as he unbuttoned her blouse and exposed her body to his gaze.

'Look at me Laura,' he breathed. 'I want to see the expression in your eyes when I take off your last garment and hold you naked in my arms.'

She obeyed drowsily, stretching like a contented cat as he flung away the blouse and paused before he tackled her black lace underwear. His own eyes were touched with fire and there was a controlled frenzy about his movements when he reached behind her and unfastened the catch on her bra. Released from their confinement, her breasts sprang free, large and lush, the nipples hard with excitement. James caught his breath at the sight and went down on one knee so that he could bury his face in their yielding warmth.

Laura felt a shudder go through her at the brush of his sleek, glossy hair on her skin and the unfamiliar, teasing caress of his warm, moist tongue. Then his mouth moved over her nipple and he began to suck rhythmically, provocatively. She gasped and arched against him, feeling as if her bones were turning to water as he shifted his position and repeated the same exquisite torment on her other breast. Then his head moved lower.

Holding the firm curve of her hips with his powerful hands, he suddenly stripped off her black silk knickers which were the last barrier between them. She caught her breath as he suddenly seized her in his arms and boosted her into the air, leaving her garments scattered carelessly on the carpet. In three swift strides he had reached the huge bed and flung her effortlessly down in the centre of it. Her heart pounded as she saw him looming over her in the lamplight with an avid, gloating expression in his eyes. His chest was heaving and his movements were swift and purposeful as he tore at his cuffs and the buttons on the front of his shirt. In an instant he was free of the confining fabric and with a muffled groan of impatience he flung it aside.

The sight of his massive shoulders and powerful chest brought an involuntary thrill to Laura, but she had little time for admiring contemplation. In a rapid series of movements James stooped and pulled off the rest of his clothes. For the first time in her life she saw a naked, fully aroused male and the sight stunned her. Her heart hammered in her throat and she had to moisten her dry lips with her tongue. He was so big, so powerful, so utterly primitive and magnificent.

As he moved towards her in a silent crouch his eyes were narrowed with desire and his features looked strange and unfamiliar, so that she experienced a moment of panic. He was beside the bed now, his knee already braced on the edge of it and the curly hairs in his groin gleaming like copper wires in the lamplight, when she suddenly caught the scent of his body. It was wild, tangy, reminiscent of salt air and leather and wood smoke. She found it unbearably arousing.

Suddenly the mattress plunged beneath the weight of his body and he was crouched above her, blocking out most of the light. She felt almost afraid, yet at the same time feverishly excited and eager. Hesitantly reaching up her hand, she stroked his cheek. Turning his head, he caught the pad of flesh at the base of her thumb between his teeth and bit it softly.

'God, I want you,' he muttered, burying his face in her neck. 'I've never wanted any woman so much in my entire life. We're going to be good together, Laura, I know we are.'

Suddenly he lowered his full weight onto her and she almost cried out in surprise. A primitive thrill of arousal tingled through her as she felt the warm, relentless pressure of his body crushing hers. His chest was so strongly muscled, his abdomen so flat and hard, his arms and legs as strong as steel cables. But most unsettling of all was that hot, hard, virile organ that was pressed against her, twitching and pulsating as if it had a separate life of its own. She moved her hips experimentally and felt a current of fire spark through her entire body. James caught his breath sharply.

'If you're going to play teasing little games like that,' he warned, 'I'm going to tease you too. Do you have sensitive ears, Laura?'

Gasping and writhing as his tongue licked them mercilessly, she discovered that she did. She also discovered that she had a sensitive throat and shoulders and breasts and belly, that her feet were unbearably erotic, that the insides of her thighs could drive her to a frenzy when tormented by James's tongue, and that the universe exploded into millions of coloured stars when he teased her in the most tantalising place of all.

'Oh, James, please... Oh, heavens, I can't... I... Oh, no more... Yes! Yes! Yes!'

With a long, moaning shudder, she contorted violently, thrusting herself against him. While the room was still spinning around her and her blood was thundering in her ears he poised himself deftly above her and gazed down at her.

'Ready to surrender?' he taunted. And took her.

She caught her breath, expecting pain, but there was none. Her body was so slick and warm from his love-play that she felt only a faint ache as he burst through her defences. And that was followed at once by a fierce gladness at the realisation that James was now thrusting deep inside her. She craved him, loved him, needed him. A blind, warm sense of completion flooded through her and she raised her hips, straining to meet him, striving for a closer, deeper union.

'I want you,' she breathed, winding her legs around him. 'I want you so badly. Oh, James, I love... I love to feel you... So strong... So-o-o-h...'

Her last words were lost in an unexpected convulsion that shook her as violently as if she were caught in an earthquake zone. James's arms tightened around her and her eyes opened briefly. She saw him gazing intently down at her, then her eyelashes fluttered shut and she surrendered once more to the dizzy, rushing exhilaration that was sweeping her along like a flash flood.

None of this was quite what she had expected. She had thought it would be rather like drifting on a quiet, dreamy lake. Instead it was more like riding over a two-mile steeplechase. But as James's heartbeat began to accelerate, and his harsh breathing filled the room, she also knew that it was the most passionate, tempestuous, fulfilling experience she had ever had in her life. Suddenly his whole body stiffened and he cried out.

'Laura!'

An answering passion whipped through her like a storm descending from a clear sky. She felt the shudder that passed through him and it wakened a deep, echoing response within her. Uttering a low moan, she clasped her arms around his neck and drew him down onto the cushion of her shoulder.

'I love you,' she breathed, and sank back, totally fulfilled.

Afterwards they lay together for a long time, not talking, but expressing their intimacy in other ways. A row of feather-light nibbling kisses along his eyebrow. A hand trailed possessively down between her breasts and into the softness at the top of her thighs. A long, crushing hug with animal growls and protesting giggles. At last James propped himself on one elbow and drew his fingers down to the sticky moisture between her thighs.

'I'm sorry about that,' he said in a serious tone. 'It was unforgivable.'

'What was?' she asked in alarm. Was he already regretting their lovemaking?

'Not using any protection. But you're quite safe. You won't catch anything.'

His frankness made her face burn scarlet.

'You won't either,' she said in a muffled voice, dropping her eyes.

'And you're all right otherwise?' he probed.

'Yes, I'm fine.'

His question baffled her. Why wouldn't she be all right? Only after she had pondered for a moment did she guess what he was really driving at. Pregnancy? With a feeling of incredulous shock, she realised that it was entirely possible. Unlikely, perhaps, but possible. Yet somehow she couldn't believe it would ever happen to her. And if it did, I'd be glad! she thought fiercely. I'd love to have your baby, James. But she didn't say any of this aloud. It was all too new, too strange, too unsettling. Instead she simply nestled her head into his shoulder and rubbed her cheek backwards and forwards against his chest.

'You shouldn't do that unless you're prepared to take the consequences,' he warned.

And, spinning her onto her back, he trapped her against the pillows and began ruthlessly to demonstrate what the consequences were.

Later still, when they lay exhausted and sated, Laura tried to analyse the implications of what had happened between them. But she was too overwhelmed by emotion to analyse anything. All she knew was that she loved James and he loved her. True, he hadn't actually told her so yet, but the message was unmistakable in the way he looked at her and held her. There were a lot of things she hadn't told him either. Like the fact that she had been a virgin. She had thought there might be physical signs, but there hadn't been. Well, time enough to-morrow to explore those delicate issues . . . A huge yawn overtook her.

James put his arms around her, rolled her onto her side and snuggled up to her spoon fashion.

'That's perfect,' he murmured, nuzzling her neck. 'Now I can stroke your breasts while you fall asleep.'

She gave a gasp of protesting laughter.

'Oh, that's guaranteed to make me doze off.'

He pinched her bottom.

'Cheeky wench! So I bored you, did I?'

'Mmm. Unbearably. Did I bore you?'

'Sweetheart, I could spend a lifetime being bored like that,' he said throatily.

A lifetime. Her heart sang. A lifetime was exactly what she wanted to spend with him.

'So, are you coming to Sue's barbecue with me?' he demanded. 'As a couple?'

Laura smiled secretly to herself.

'If you insist,' she murmured.

*   *   *

The party was already in full swing when James and Laura arrived at Sue's house the following day. As they parked their car half a block away they could already smell the aroma of frying steak, hear the blare of music, the clink of glasses and the sound of upraised laughter. It was a glorious, sunny day, and even the coolness of Sue's greeting couldn't dampen Laura's happiness. Besides, once they had escaped from their hostess's clutches, she found herself surrounded by a throng of familiar figures. All the people who had attended Bea's wedding were there, and she was soon being offered food and drinks and being drawn into the latest gossip.

To her delight, James hovered beside her with one arm possessively around her waist, and even when he went across to the buffet tables under the trees to fetch her a glass of champagne his gaze sought hers and he gave her a special, secret smile. As he returned with the two glass flutes full of bubbling, golden liquid, the bush band struck up a lively tune.

'This is fun, isn't it?' said Laura.

James bent his head close to her ear so that he could not be heard by anyone else above the uproar of the music.

'Yes, but I'd rather be at home with you, naked, in bed.'

Laura blushed and dropped her eyes. At that moment, she heard a muffled crash followed by a cry of annoyance from the brick patio overlooking the garden. Looking up, she saw Sue on her knees amid a mess of broken glass and potato salad. A twinge of guilt stabbed through her. Had it been the sight of her and James which had made Sue drop the bowl? She made a swift decision and thrust her champagne glass into James's hand.

'Sue's dropped something,' she said. 'I'm just going over to her.

'Can I help you?' she asked, stepping onto the patio.

Sue's green eyes were suspiciously bright and her chin was quivering as she looked up from her task of gathering shards of broken glass.

'No, you can't,' she snapped. 'The only help you can give me is to get the hell out of here. Oh, you think you're so clever, don't you? But it won't last; I promise you that! It never does with James. He makes you think you're the most wonderful, special person in the world and then—oh, God, I hate you!'

With a sudden, strangled sob, Sue abandoned the scene of the disaster and fled inside. Not knowing what else to do, Laura stooped down and went on with the task of clearing up. She had just finished gathering all the fragments of broken glass into a pile and was beginning to lift the clotted lumps of potato salad with a paper napkin when Wendy Fraser appeared beside her with a plastic rubbish bin and a dustpan and brush.

'What was that all about?' she asked curiously. 'I saw Sue drop the bowl and you come to help her, but she looked as if she was shouting at you.'

'She was warning me off James,' replied Laura unhappily.

'Oh, dear. Poor Sue,' said Wendy, sweeping up the pile of glass and tossing it into the bin. 'So she's been given her marching orders, has she? Well, it was bound to happen, I suppose. But I didn't think she'd be as upset as that about it.'

'Do you think I should go after her?' asked Laura in a worried voice.

'No, you'll only make matters worse,' advised Wendy, taking the last messy bundle of potato salad from her and offering her a paper napkin to wipe her hands. 'Anyway, I don't know why she bothered trying to warn you off. You're not fool enough to fall for him, are you?'

Laura remained silent, but evidently her face revealed everything, for James's sister gave her a pitying look and shook her head.

'I don't see why you all have to carry on as if he's Bluebeard!' burst out Laura. 'Is it entirely beyond the bounds of possibility that James might fall genuinely in love with someone?'

'Yes,' said Wendy bluntly. 'Look, Laura, it's all very well to have an affair with him, but for heaven's sake don't lose your head. Or your heart. You'll regret it if you do. I'm fond of James, and there's nobody I'd rather have on my side if the chips were down, but there's no denying that he can be an utter bastard in some ways.'

'Are you talking about me?' murmured a resonant masculine voice.

Laura and Wendy jumped as James appeared beside them. He had crept up as silently as a hunting cat, taking them both by surprise.

'I was warning her off you,' announced Wendy defiantly. 'I like Laura, and I don't fancy watching you eat her up for supper. I think the kindest thing you could do is leave her alone, James.' Picking up the rubbish bin, she looked directly at Laura. 'Take my advice and look after yourself.'

James gave an exasperated snort as Wendy vanished into the house.

'Hell's teeth,' he grumbled. 'With sisters like that, who needs enemies? What did she say to you, anyway?'

Laura took the champagne glass which he was holding out to her and took a large gulp for courage. The liquid seemed to fizz like fire through her veins.

'She was warning me that you're the big bad wolf and that little pigs like me should watch out.'

'Wendy's the one who should watch out,' growled James. 'She should also mind her own damned business! I don't know where she gets off, calling me the big bad wolf, seeing that she's never lasted six months in a relationship with anyone.'

'And you have?' challenged Laura.

James ground his teeth.

'No, but that's not to say that I can't. It's just that I haven't met the right woman.'

'Until now?' demanded Laura. She'd meant it to sound like a cynical joke, but her voice came out with an embarrassing wobble.

James scrutinised her with a keen, appraising stare.

'Perhaps,' he said, half to himself. 'I'm not sure yet, but I certainly don't want Wendy shooting me down in flames before I have a chance to find out.'

Laura bit her lip. Well, if he was prepared to give the relationship a chance, that was better than nothing. But a feeling of bitter disappointment crept through her. She was already certain in her own heart that James was the right one for her, or she would never have made love with him last night. She had thought he felt the same way about her and it was a shock to discover that he was still wavering.

'I see,' she muttered, avoiding his eyes.

With a low growl of exasperation, James seized both the champagne flutes and set them down impatiently on the table. Then he seized her by the shoulders and thrust his face close to hers.

'Don't look so damned pitiful!' he urged. 'You'll lay yourself wide open to exploitation if you show your feelings as easily as that. You need to be tougher and harder, Laura. People will hurt you if you wear your heart on your sleeve.'

'They won't if they're decent people!'

'Yes, but how many people are?'

The sneering tone in his voice was unmistakable, but she tried hard to remain calm, not to let him see how hurt she was.

'Are you telling me that I'm throwing myself at you?' she demanded hoarsely. 'Are you saying that you don't want to see me any more?'

She saw the flash of annoyance in his eyes.

'I didn't say that!' he protested. 'I just think that you ought to protect yourself better. You're far too naïve and trusting.'

'Is that what I was being last night?' she demanded bitterly. 'You know, it's a funny thing, but I thought it was safe to trust you, James. I didn't realise that I was being naïve by thinking something special was happening between us.'

'There is something special happening between us!'

'Then why are you trying to push me off?'

He gritted his teeth and gave a long, shuddering sigh.

'I'm not trying to push you off. I'm just trying to... Oh, hell, Laura, what do you think is going on between us? What do you want from me?'

She knew she might be about to make a bigger fool of herself than she ever had in her life before, but she decided to take the risk anyway.

'I've fallen in love with you,' she said unsteadily. 'And it's the most amazing thing that's ever happened to me in my life. What I want is to get to know you better and give the relationship a chance. I'm not asking you to marry me, James—not yet, anyway. But I do want you to take me seriously and not play games with me. That's all.'

His whole body was as rigid as if he were frozen in ice. Even his eyes didn't flicker and he scarcely seemed to breathe. The silence seemed to lengthen agonisingly between them until at last he spoke.

'You make me feel totally ashamed of myself.'

Laura stared at him in dismay.

'What's that supposed to mean? Are you saying that Wendy and Sue are right about you? That you are only playing games with me?'

'No,' muttered James. 'It just means that your honesty and courage blow me away... Look, Laura, you're the one with all the certainties about what's happening between us. What do you want to do next?'

She stared at him, uncertain whether to feel hope or despair. But hadn't he just said that she was brave and honest? Then shouldn't she be prepared to risk being hurt or humiliated by saying what she really did want?

'I want us to spend more time together. I have to go back to Sydney in three weeks' time or I'll lose my job and have no way of supporting myself. I thought perhaps you could come up and visit me for a while.'

He was silent for a moment, staring at her with a brooding expression. Then he raised his hand and touched her cheek.

'I'll think about it,' he promised. 'I'll think about every possible way of handling the situation. And let's begin by getting out of here.'

He remained silent nearly all the way home in the car, although once he reached across and gripped her hand so hard that it hurt. When he'd stopped the car inside the garage, he turned and looked at her.

'About this Sydney visit—' he began.

Somewhere inside the house, the telephone rang.

'Damn!' exclaimed James. 'Look, I'll go. We'll talk about it once we're inside.'

It took her a moment to gather up their jackets and lock the doors of the garage before she followed him inside. It must have been a very short phone call, for the house already seemed completely hushed. James was nowhere near the telephone in the hall, but she went from door to door looking for him and found him at last in the living room. He was standing at the window, with his back to her. His head was bowed and his shoulders were ominously still.

'Well? What did you decide about Sydney?' Her throat was unaccountably dry and she felt a premonition of disaster as he swung round to face her. He gave a harsh, croaking laugh and his golden eyes were pitiless.

'Sorry, Laura. I'm not coming. I've enjoyed our little fling, but it's time to call it quits. The game is over.'

Dr Williamson's office seemed exactly the same as usual, with the framed photo of his wife and two university student sons on the wall, the muffled sound of the telephone ringing in the receptionist's office at the end of the corridor, the clutter of medical journals on the shelves and the smell of antiseptic that hung in the air. Even the worn patch of leather on the chair was poking through Laura's tights in exactly the same way as usual.

It was hard to believe that something so dramatic could be happening in such an ordinary place. But she had been back in Sydney for a month now and she had good reason to be apprehensive. She held her breath as Dr Williamson screwed up his red face and frowned at the Petri dish in his hands.

'Well?' she demanded.

He gave a long, meditative sigh.

'It's positive, I'm afraid. But you didn't need me to tell you that, did you? You've got all the symptoms. Two weeks overdue, tingling breasts, nausea in the mornings.'

'Then I'm really going to have a baby?' asked Laura shakily.

'That is the usual result of pregnancy, yes.'

An extraordinary tumult of emotions surged through her. Disbelief, dismay, terror and an unexpected flash of total delight.

'I—I can't believe it,' she stammered.

'And I can't believe you didn't think of this sooner,' said the doctor disapprovingly, rising to his feet and going over to the sink to wash his hands. He tore off a strip of paper towelling and turned back to her, scowling sternly. 'You're not a sixteen-year-old with no under-standing of how your body works. Why on earth didn't you take precautions?'

'I didn't come here for a lecture!' flared Laura. 'I just came here to find out the truth.'

Keith Williamson sat down again and eyed her over the top of his glasses.

'Well, now you know it, you're going to have to decide pretty smartly what you intend to do. Is there any prospect of marriage?'

Laura felt a sickening lurch of horror as she remembered that last unbearable scene with James and her frantic escape to Sydney. She had spent most of the last month in tears of rage or misery, barely able to function because of her grief and disillusionment. He had told her he never wanted to see her again and the feeling was entirely mutual.

Marriage? Never! Although, ironically enough, she could still marry Raymond Hall if she chose to do so. On her very first day back in Sydney Ray had come round to her house and renewed his proposal, and even her admission that she had had an affair with another man had not deterred him. But she didn't love Ray and she had no intention of foisting someone else's baby on him. She shook her head.

'No,' she said miserably.

The doctor sighed and reached for a booking pad.

'In that case I suppose you'll want to consider a termination?'

'No!' Her misery was transformed to shock and outrage. She crossed her hands protectively over her body. 'I couldn't possibly do that! I'm going to have this baby and keep it.'

'Laura,' said the doctor wearily, 'you've been my patient for a very long time and I want you to think seriously about this. Have you ever considered how hard it is to be a single mother?'

'Well, we're in the nineteen nineties now, not the Dark Ages!' retorted Laura defiantly. 'Lots of women do it.'

'And lots of women have a hard and lonely time of it! Even if you can manage emotionally, it won't be easy from a practical point of view. And I'm warning you now, your firm won't be too happy about it. I know there are laws about discrimination, but they're an old-fashioned conservative lot where you work, and it won't do any good to your career.'

'Stuff the firm!'

Dr Williamson blinked.

'Perhaps adoption—' he began.

'No!' She was on her feet now and shouting. 'I won't have an abortion and I won't give up my baby. And if my firm doesn't want to employ me any more, I'll go elsewhere!'

Dr Williamson scratched his head.

'Well, you'll find it very difficult combining a baby and a full-time job wherever you go. Is there any chance the child's father could help you?'

'No!' choked Laura, clenching her fists. 'Don't even mention it! Nobody can help me. I'm completely on my own.'

CHAPTER SEVEN

'GARETH, it's time for your nap!'

'No!' shouted the toddler joyfully, and took off at full pelt down the garden.

Laura caught him up as he was trying to wriggle beneath the plumbago bush near the sandpit, and lifted him kicking and squealing into her arms. She really had been lucky finding a job in this small town in Queensland, where she could afford to rent a house with a garden—even if it did mean that Gareth spent most of his time looking like a sandminer. She gazed down fondly at his riotous brown curls, blue eyes, chubby cheeks and sturdy limbs.

At just under two years of age, he didn't resemble James in the slightest. In fact, he looked exactly like Laura's mother. Even so, she could never catch a glimpse of him without feeling a sharp pang of regret that brought back memories of his father. But, however much pain he had caused her, Gareth was also the greatest joy of her life.

She carried him inside to the bathroom and he giggled and twisted as she washed the sand off his hands and feet. He also hampered her efforts by trying to play pat-a-cake and singing.

'This a way a farmer wide, Hobby gee, Hobby gee, Hobby gee.'

Laura smiled and began to chant obligingly.

> This is the way the farmer rides
> Hobbledy gee
> Hobbledy gee
> Hobbledy gee
> This is the way the lady rides
> Trippety trip
> Trippety trip
> Trippety trip...

The rollicking rhythm of the song brought back the memory of horses' hooves thudding along a sandy beach. For an instant she was transported into another world of pounding breakers, howling winds and a tall, black-haired man on a cavorting horse. She faltered and fell silent, staring into the distance. Gareth nudged her.

'This a way a li'l boy wide, Tumba dow, dow, dow,' he prompted.

She smiled mistily at him. 'Yes, darling.

> This is the way the little boy rides
> Cloppity clop
> Cloppity clop
> Cloppity clop
> Tumble down, down, down.'

She tipped him backwards off her lap, shrieking with delight, then hauled him back up and kissed him.

'Come on. Bed.'

Carrying him upstairs, she tucked him into his cot and paused for a moment in the darkened room to cherish the sight of him snuggling up to his teddy. It's a bad habit, hanging around like this when he's trying to go to sleep, she told herself. I'm probably spoiling him, but he's all I've got except for Bea, and I don't see Bea much these days.

She glanced up at the photo on the wall, which was a colour portrait of Sam, Bea, Laura and James outside the church on Bea's wedding day. Laura would have preferred to have a photo without James, but Bea had brought this one with her on her visit last Christmas and Gareth had taken a fancy to it, insisting that it be hung on his bedroom wall. Following Laura's gaze, he pulled his thumb out of his mouth with a pop and pointed at the photo.

'Auntie Bea a pwincess,' he announced.

'No, not a princess, a bride.'

'Mummy a bwide too.'

'No, Gareth, Mummy's not a bride.'

'Mummy a bwide, Sam a bwide, James a bwide!' insisted Gareth loudly.

Halfway between laughter and tears, Laura retreated to the door.

'Go to sleep,' she ordered.

Downstairs in the kitchen she made herself a cup of coffee and sat sipping the hot, fragrant liquid and staring reflectively at the coils of steam that rose from it.

'I wish I could get rid of that photo,' she said aloud. 'I hate having to see James every time I go into Gareth's room.'

Then she gave herself a small, impatient shake and reached for a seed catalogue. She must stop being so self-pitying. Really she had been incredibly lucky. Gareth was healthy and lively and she had fallen on her feet by finding this job and house in Queensland.

After she had discovered that she was pregnant, she had resigned from her firm in Sydney, let out her flat and travelled north. Feeling that her life was spinning wildly out of control, she had decided to do the one thing she had always wanted and had travelled around visiting the national parks and botanical gardens. It had been a chance event which had brought her this part-time job, when she had seen an advertisement for a bookkeeper in a local nursery. Now she was firmly settled here on the Sunshine Coast and all her dreams had come true. Almost.

'Well, eternal love is probably a myth anyway,' she said bitterly. 'And at least I've recovered from James.'

The telephone rang. For some reason Laura felt a prickling sense of uneasiness, although she told herself that it was probably only Barbara, the owner of the nursery. She often dropped by for coffee on a Sunday afternoon. Picking up the receiver, she strove to speak calmly.

'Hello?'

'Laura? This is James Fraser.'

Her heart almost stopped at the shock of hearing that familiar voice after so long. Had she really thought she was over it? What a fool she was! Her unsteady breathing and fluttering pulse told her she would never be over it. Then her initial astonishment was followed by frantic alarm as she realised that James would not have con-tacted her unless something serious had happened.

'Is something wrong?' she demanded sharply.

'Yes, I'm afraid there is. Bea and Sam have had a car accident.'

Her legs seemed to go from under her and there was a roaring noise in her ears as the room spun round her. Clutching at a kitchen chair for support, she slid down against the wall and sat on the floor with her legs stiffly extended like a wooden doll's. Bea? No, not Bea! There must be some mistake. Bea couldn't be badly hurt—not crazy, lovable Bea, who had always been more alive than anyone else. Dear God, it was impossible! A sudden, choking sob caught in her throat. James's voice buzzed in her ear as if from a great distance.

'Laura, are you there? Laura, answer me! Are you all right?'

What would he care? she thought savagely. Fighting for control, she wiped away the hot salt tears that were sliding down her cheeks and forced herself to speak.

'Yes, I'm here. James, how bad is it? Tell me the truth.'

She could hear the rising note of panic in her voice and then James's reply came back, cool and bracing.

'It's bad, Laura, but they're not dead, either of them. They're both in Intensive Care with fractures, and the doctors are afraid Bea's broken her neck.'

'Broken her neck? Oh, God! You don't mean ... she could be paralysed?'

'We're not sure about anything yet, except that we need you down here as soon as possible. Can you come?'

'Of course,' she said feverishly. Her gaze tracked wildly round the room. 'But I'll have to organise flights, money...'

'I've already done that. Now, listen carefully—have you got a pen? I've booked you on a flight from Maroochydore at five past six this evening and it gets into Melbourne shortly after ten p.m. You stay overnight at the Airport Travelodge and catch the first flight to Hobart tomorrow morning at eight-fifteen, arriving at nine-twenty. I'll meet you at the airport in Tasmania. Have you got all that?'

'Yes,' said Laura through frozen lips. Her brain was already leaping ahead to the subject of Gareth, suitcases, warm clothes for the Tasmanian winter, then it swung wildly back to the thought of Bea. Bea! Would she be in time to see her? What if the worst happened? And Sam—she had forgotten all about Sam! How badly hurt was Bea's husband? 'James, what about Sam? How's he?'

'Not well,' said James in a matter-of-fact voice. 'But not as bad as Bea. He has broken ribs, a punctured lung and a fractured fibula, but he's conscious and expected to make a full recovery. I'll tell you the details when I see you tomorrow.'

'All right,' she agreed with a shaky sigh. 'Thank you for calling me.'

'I'm sorry to be the bearer of bad news,' he said roughly. 'I know how upsetting this must be for you, but you've always been brave, Laura, so don't fail us now. I'll see you tomorrow.'

Laura hung up the receiver and howled. All the time that she was making frenzied dashes around the house, hauling suitcases out of cupboards and clothes out of drawers, she kept crying bitterly. She only managed to stop long enough to phone her boss, Barbara, and ask her to keep an eye on the house and organise a replacement bookkeeper.

While she was cleaning out the refrigerator and pouring milk down the sink she suddenly went to pieces completely. She was still gulping and hiccuping when she heard a muffled thump overhead, followed by the sound of footsteps. Moments later a small, solid figure cannoned into her thigh and chubby arms hugged her violently.

'What's wong, Mummy?'

'Gareth! How did you get out of bed?'

'Gaweth cwimb out,' he announced proudly. 'Mummy cwying. Hurt aself?'

He peered anxiously at her knees for signs of bloodstains and then looked up at her. The sight of those wide blue eyes brought her back to her senses. People were depending on her—she couldn't just crack up! Seizing a length of paper towel, she tore it off and scrubbed her face with it, then gave him a watery smile.

'I'm better now, darling. Would you like to come for a trip on a plane with Mummy?'

The need to take care of her son helped her through that nightmare journey, even though she was so frustrated by the slowness of the flight that she longed to jump out and push. When they reached Melbourne late at night the homely, familiar task of giving Gareth a bath and getting him into bed gave her something to take her mind off her own desperate anxiety. Only when the blue waters of Bass Strait appeared beneath the wings of the plane the following morning and the first mountain peaks of Tasmania began to rear up ahead of them did her fears come hurtling back in full force.

Poor Bea! She had thought she was coming to this island to live happily ever after, and now look what had happened! Staring down at the jagged blue peaks with their covering of white snow, Laura remembered Bea's radiant joy on her wedding day and could not suppress the host of other memories that accompanied the thought. Memories of James... Not that it mattered. Nothing mattered now, except that Bea and her husband should recover from their injuries. Even the thought of confronting James in person no longer had the power to hurt Laura as it might once have done.

A cold wind was whipping across the tarmac and rain was falling in a steady drizzle as she came down the front stairs of the plane. Exhausted by his long journey the previous day, Gareth had dozed off and was lying like a log across her shoulder, so that she had to struggle with him and a folding pushchair and an overnight bag.

Luckily a middle-aged man came to her aid. Overriding her protests, he hoisted Gareth into his arms and took the pushchair, leaving Laura with the overnight bag.

'Put your head down and we'll make a run for the terminal,' he advised.

James was waiting just inside the building, wearing a dark cashmere coat that made him look extremely sombre. Laura had rehearsed this scene in her mind a million times, but she had never imagined that it would be like this. Even though she thought she hated him, she could not suppress a treacherous rush of relief at the sight of him, and with a low cry she ran forward and flung herself into his arms.

In spite of the grim expression on his face, he gripped her tightly. Once again she had the ridiculous feeling that he was as safe and unchangeable as a rock, that he would give her shelter and protection, no matter what went wrong. Gazing up at him, she saw that his black hair, tawny eyes and hawk-like features looked the same as ever, although he was more haggard than she had ever seen him.

'How are they?' she demanded urgently.

'There's no change, but don't give up hope. Let's find your suitcases and we'll get out of here.'

A man cleared his throat beside her, and she turned to see the passenger who had helped her off the plane.

'Here's your little boy,' he said kindly. 'Can you and your husband manage now?'

Laura winced inwardly at his assumption that she was married to James, but she did not think it worth explaining.

'Yes, we'll be fine,' she replied, reaching out her arms and taking the sleeping child from him. 'Thank you for your help.'

She realised that James was staring down at Gareth with an appalled expression on his face. Had he guessed the truth? Her heart began to hammer violently.

'Is this your son?' he asked hoarsely.

'Yes.' She might have added, And yours, but she didn't. Surely he would guess, in any case. Who else's child could it be? Was it really likely that she would have had an affair with James while she was expecting somebody else's baby? Or did he think she had conceived Gareth after they had parted? If only he would say something, *anything*.

She looked at him, trying to read his thoughts in his face, but, as always, James was completely inscrutable. His lips tightened with some indefinable emotion, but she couldn't guess what he was feeling. Anger? Jealousy? Indifference? Contempt? At last he shrugged, as if dismissing the issue.

'I see,' he said in clipped tones. 'Well, you'd better assemble that pushchair thing and get him comfortable while I look for the suitcases. Can you describe them to me?'

Laura stared at him in amazement, unable to believe that he had dismissed the subject of Gareth so easily. True, they were in a public place, and she certainly had no intention of going into details here herself, yet James had given no hint of wanting to tackle the matter later. It was as if it held absolutely no importance for him. She felt her own anger surge so that it threatened to choke her, but she vowed to match his indifference with her own. Her voice was as cold and clipped as his when she replied.

'They're medium-sized, tan, and there are two of them. And a plastic car seat as well.'

As soon as he'd found them he picked them up and set off for the car park, with his head down and his long legs covering the ground in gigantic strides. It reminded her of the way he had walked angrily away from her on the beach when he'd still thought that she was Bea. Once again she had to run to catch up with him, but this time the gulf of bitterness and betrayal that settled between them was completely unbridgeable.

She watched his scowl as he paid for the parking ticket and her heart sank. He still seemed to hate her as much as ever, but why? Why? Surely if there was any hating to be done she was the one who had a right to do it? Hadn't he hurt her far worse than she had ever hurt him? Or did he think that his action in seducing and abandoning her was a just revenge for her initial deceit? She flashed him a bitter, smouldering look as she lifted Gareth out of his pushchair and felt him snuggle into her neck. Settling him tenderly into the car seat and adjusting the seat belt, she kissed him on the cheek.

She was just going to climb in beside him when she saw that James was holding the front door open for her. Reluctantly she took her place in the front seat beside him.

'Wasn't your husband free to come with you?' asked James as they drove away from the car park.

'I don't have a husband.'

'You mean you're already divorced?' The disapproval in his tone was unmistakable.

'No, I mean I'm unmarried.'

His eyebrows drew together.

'So you deserted that accountant chap of yours, did you?'

Laura gave him a startled glance. So that was it! Obviously he thought that Gareth was Raymond's son, which meant that Bea must have told him about Raymond, in spite of her promise never to discuss her sister with James.

'Yes, if you want to put it that way,' she agreed coldly. 'How about you? Are you married?'

'No.'

The monosyllable was little more than a throaty growl.

'I thought perhaps you and Sue—'

'Sue got divorced and is now remarried happily and living in Western Australia.'

Laura felt an absurd pang of relief that made her want to kick herself. What did it matter to her whether James and Sue had got married? She was never going to have any more to do with him in any case!

'What happened about the shopping centre?' she asked, trying to change the subject.

'We blocked it,' said James.

His eyes were stony and his jaw looked as solid and unyielding as a lump of granite, so that Laura had to suppress a half-hysterical urge to burst into laughter. Of course he'd blocked it! The developers should have known that they couldn't cross James Fraser and get away with it! They might as well try to struggle with a solid cliff-face.

'How's everyone else in the village?' she asked.

James shrugged.

'The same as ever, but I won't bore you with the details. It wouldn't mean much to an outsider.'

An outsider. Thanks very much for the reminder, James! Well, it's a good thing you're not bothering with small talk because I didn't come here to be friends with you, you swine. I came here to help my sister.

'What do the doctors say about Bea and Sam?' she asked abruptly.

'They're seriously worried about Bea. Apparently the X-rays of her neck show a line across the second vertebra which shouldn't be there.'

'Well, what does it mean?'

James's face looked grim.

'It could mean that she has a fracture of the odontoid process—or, in layman's language, a hangman's fracture. If that's so, then merely turning her head could be enough to make her die instantly.'

'What? But don't they know for sure? Are they completely useless? What the hell's happening? Aren't they doing anything for her?'

She could hear the mounting hysteria in her own voice and was almost grateful when James's hand reached across and crushed hers.

'Laura,' he said sternly. 'They're doing everything they can for her. At the moment they're trying to get her condition stabilised enough to move her to another hospital tomorrow. Once she's there, they'll do a CAT scan and we should know what's happening. Until then you can't do Bea or anyone else any good by cracking up. Do you understand?'

Laura nodded and clutched her handbag tightly, struggling not to give way to hysteria. She would just have to be patient and hope for good news soon, but the waiting threatened to be unbearable.

'Who was driving the car?' she burst out at last.

'Bea was, but the accident wasn't her fault. A drunken driver lost control on a bend and hit them. Needless to say, he escaped with only minor cuts and abrasions.'

'How unfair!'

'Life's unfair.'

As they approached the centre of the city Laura's thoughts were given a welcome diversion, when Gareth suddenly woke up and began bouncing energetically at the sight of fishing boats and seagulls in the docks.

'Boats!' he cried gleefully. 'Ducks!'

He tried to undo his seat belt and climb out.

'Gareth, stop that!' cried Laura. 'Sit properly in your seat. I'll take you for a walk as soon as we get to where we're staying. James, I haven't discussed the matter of accommodation with you. Do you know of a hotel anywhere that would suit us?'

James glanced over his shoulder at Gareth, who was now trying to squirm underneath the seat belt to make his escape.

'I did have you booked in at the casino hotel—at my expense, of course—but I think that lively little customer in the back seat might be better off staying at Bea and Sam's house. There's a garden there, the beach is close by and you could do whatever cooking you feel like. Would that suit you?'

Laura looked at him with relief. She had never liked hotels, and at the moment the last thing she wanted to do was deal with strangers.

'All right,' she agreed. 'Thank you.'

She felt a twinge of dismay as the car pulled up in the driveway of the house where she had first met James, but if he was sharing her bittersweet memories he gave no sign of it. Lifting the luggage out of the car, he led the way to the front door.

'When can we go to the hospital and see them?' asked Laura.

'As soon as you've had some coffee and settled in,' he said, ushering her into the hallway. 'Just choose whatever rooms you want for the two of you. I'm in the green bedroom next to Sam and Bea's at the moment, but I'm quite happy to have another one if you'd prefer that.'

A chill settled in the pit of her stomach.

'You mean you're staying here too?'

'Yes, but don't worry. I won't be making any advances to you.'

Until now James had been more or less polite, but this time there was no mistaking the contemptuous sneer in his voice. Laura's nerves were already frayed by worry and exhaustion, and her anger ignited like a blowtorch.

'That's just as well,' she said venomously. 'You wouldn't get far.'

Their eyes met and hatred surged between them as lethally as a high voltage current. For two pins she would have walked straight back out of this house and climbed on a plane to return to Queensland, but she couldn't do that because of Bea. Well, she might have to stay here, but that didn't mean she would have to like it!

What infuriated her most about the whole situation was James's unfairness. As she saw it, she was the injured party, not him, so what right did he have to glare at her as if she were something nasty stuck to the bottom of his shoe? He was a brute and a heartless, shallow, exploitative swine, and she would like to kill him! Her fists clenched, her breast heaved and her breath came in rapid shallow flutters as she glared angrily back at him. It was all she could do to stop herself from slapping his face and shouting at him, hurling all the reproaches at him which had simmered inside her for almost three years.

The force of her rage was almost exhilarating, but to her dismay she saw signs of similar tension in James himself. His narrowed eyes, his grimly set mouth, the muscle that was twitching in his cheek as if his teeth were gritted, the white outline of his knuckles clenched on the handles of her suitcases all hinted at a pent-up hostility just as fierce as her own. While they stood motionless in this stalemate Laura suddenly felt an urgent tug on her coat.

'Gaweth go potty. Now!'

She knew from experience that it was unwise to ignore that summons. Casting a final, burning look at James, she rushed her son into the bathroom. When they emerged, she heard the sound of coffee-cups clattering in the kitchen.

'Laura,' called James in a cool, controlled voice. 'Come here, please.'

She obeyed resentfully and found him setting the kitchen table with a completely serene expression on his face.

'I'm sorry if I said anything to offend you,' he said. 'And I'll offer to move out if you think it will be too desperately awkward for us to remain under the same roof, but I won't deny that it would cause me difficulties. I'll have to take over Sam's job at the woollen mill while he's laid up and a lot of his files and computer disks are here in this house. It would be a huge job to move them.'

'I can hardly turn you out of the place,' replied Laura stiffly.

'Good,' said James, smiling at her with that faintly wolfish baring of his teeth which had once sent tremors of arousal down her spine. 'Then let's do our best to get along together. After all, what happened between us is over and done with and no longer very important, so we ought to be able to have civilised dealings with each other. I'll promise to be pleasant if you will. Agreed?'

'Agreed,' she muttered, accepting his outstretched hand.

All the same, a pang of resentment went through her at his curt dismissal of their shared involvement as something unimportant that belonged to the past. If I told you Gareth was your son, would you still think it was unimportant and belonging only to the past? she wondered bitterly.

A strange feeling seized her as she watched James squat down on the floor with a biscuit tin and solemnly offer Gareth one of the chocolate sticks in it. Gareth was already chattering away a mile a minute in his usual garbled lingo and there was a glint of amusement in James's eyes as he listened, which disturbed her deeply. No, she would never tell him the secret of Gareth's parentage out of mere spite. But what if there were good reasons for doing so? Did she really have the right to deprive Gareth of all contact with his father?

So far he had been little more than a baby, and it hadn't mattered much to him. But what about the years ahead? And what about James himself? Even if he had treated her abominably, did that mean he had no right to any contact with his son? Yet if she did tell him the truth, what would the results of her honesty be? Would he simply reject Gareth as he had rejected her, or would there be access visits, trips backwards and forwards between Tasmania and Queensland? That would mean years of inevitable contact between her and James and she simply couldn't bear it. It would tear her in two. A wave of faintness swept over her at the mere thought.

'Are you all right?' demanded James curtly. 'You look ill.'

'It's just tiredness and worry,' she said. 'I'll be better once I've seen Bea.'

A twinge of guilt attacked her at the realisation that she had completely forgotten about Bea for the last ten minutes, but as she sipped the fragrant, reviving coffee her thoughts turned from her own troubles to her sister's.

The hospital looked as bleak as Laura's mood, with puddles of rain lying in shiny mirrors around the car park and bare black tree branches poking up from sodden green lawns. James settled her and Gareth in the waiting room and went off to see if he could speak to a doctor. He returned shaking his head.

'No more information, I'm afraid. But they'll let you see her for a short time.'

Nothing could have prepared her for the sight of Bea looking so frail and defenceless in the high bed. There were sandbags packed around her head and some kind of stiff collar on her neck and her eyes were closed. Laura wasn't sure that her sister could hear her, but she held her hand and spoke to her in a whisper.

'Bea, it's Laura and Gareth here. Please get well soon. We all love you so much. You've got to fight, sweetheart—'

Her voice broke and she couldn't go on. She swallowed hard, trying to blink back tears in order not to frighten Gareth. To her astonishment she suddenly found her hand crushed in James's larger one. She clung to him silently, grateful for the comfort of his grip. Later, when they had visited Sam and were standing in the car park, he looked at her with a deep, scrutinising gaze which puzzled her. But when he spoke his voice was matter-of-fact.

'We'll go and have some lunch, then I'll take you both home for a rest.'

They went to Mure's fish house on the waterfront, so that Gareth could see the boats and the 'ducks'. While he pressed his nose against the window pane and gazed at the harbour outside the two adults talked.

As if by some silent agreement, they avoided the subject of Bea and Sam's accident and discussed other things: films, travel, the woollen mill, Laura's new home in Queensland. She felt as if James were drawing her away from the edge of a dark and terrifying abyss, and was thankful for his reassuring presence. Yet she also felt ashamed of her own readiness to lean on him. When they had finished their fried scallops, chips and salad, he ordered sweet black coffee without consulting her.

'Are you feeling better now?' he asked. 'You've got more colour in your cheeks.'

'Yes. Thank you. I'm sorry to go to pieces like this. I shouldn't be letting you carry all the problems on your own.'

'That's rubbish, Laura,' he said sharply. 'You're the one with the greater burden to bear at the moment. Fond as I am of Bea these days, my feelings are nothing compared to your attachment to her. Besides, where would the world be if we couldn't show a little kindness to each other in times of trouble?'

Laura's chin quivered as she looked back at him, and she wished despairingly that she could fathom what was going on in his mind. James had been so cruel to her in the past—why was he being so nice now?

It was a question which continued to haunt her in the days that followed. To their mutual joy the specialist phoned James with the welcome news that Bea did not have a broken neck, but only a whiplash injury. Although she still faced several weeks in hospital, she was expected to make a complete recovery. They had barely absorbed that joyful message when they learned that Sam had developed pneumonia in his punctured lung, and there was more shared anxiety to face.

But soon life began to settle into a routine, where their worries were balanced by the need to tackle daily chores. Each morning James went to work at the mill while Laura played with Gareth and looked after the house. In the afternoons she hired a babysitter so that she could go to the hospital and in the evenings they all ate dinner together and visited the invalids again. In many ways it was like being a family and Laura found the experience alarmingly addictive.

To her dismay she found that she was looking forward to James's return from work each evening. Worse still, she realised that Gareth was becoming deeply attached to him. The moment he heard James's key in the front door, he would fly to meet him and the pair would hold long, garbled conversations while Laura put dinner on the table. On the weekends James often took the little boy into the garden to play soccer, or read him stories in front of the fire. Laura watched their growing attachment with a feeling of deep uneasiness.

Matters came to a head one Saturday about a month after their arrival from Queensland. It was to be Gareth's birthday on the Tuesday and James had offered to take him for a walk around the Salamanca markets while Laura shopped for his present. At about eleven o'clock she emerged from a toy shop in the city with a fireman's outfit concealed in her shopping bag and walked down to meet them both at a street café in the market.

'Did you have a good time?' she asked, slipping into a chair with a sigh of relief and resting her aching feet.

Gareth beamed at her through a milkshake moustache.

'Saw a clown got a wed nose. Balloon go pop. Eat chicken muggets!' he babbled.

James met her eyes with an ironical smile.

'Gareth saw a clown with a red nose. His balloon went pop and he ate chicken nuggets,' he translated.

'Heavens, I thought I was the only one who understood what he said!'

'Ah, but I have a PhD in childspeak,' retorted James, ruffling the child's hair.

Laura suddenly sat motionless, her hand frozen halfway to the menu, unable to take her eyes off the pair of them. James's gesture, so natural and affectionate, troubled her deeply. And with a painful flash of insight, she realised that it wasn't only the question of telling him the truth which was worrying her, it was the way she felt about him. I still love him, she thought despairingly. Heaven help me, I still love him. The brute! How can I be such a fool?

'Are you going to have something to eat or drink?' asked James, beginning to look at her with an attentive frown.

She had always had the uneasy feeling that he could read her mind, and she knew that any moment now he would begin asking probing questions that she didn't want to answer. She forced herself to smile and look carefree.

'Just a cappuccino, thanks.'

Taking deep, calming breaths, she tried to control her agitation by looking around at the marketplace. There was plenty to see, with the bustle of brightly clad tourists milling around against the backdrop of honey-coloured sandstone warehouses as they examined leather handbags, home-made jewellery, curly green cabbages and secondhand books.

She tried to pay attention to the uproar of buskers playing guitars and stallholders chanting their wares, to the smell of frying samosas and Greek souvlaki, to the hum of life and pleasure which filled the air. But it was useless. Each time she saw another family drifting by with a baby in a carrier, or a child skipping between two parents, she felt as if a knife had been plunged into her heart. Why couldn't she have that sort of simple happiness? To an outsider it might look as if she did, but she and Gareth and James would soon be scattered again and she would be lonelier than ever. How could she bear it?

'Shouldn't we go home?' she asked abruptly, rising to her feet.

James looked at his watch.

'All right.'

She was silent on the drive home, busy with her thoughts, but when they opened the front door she was jolted out of her listlessness by a sudden, full-throated shout.

'Surprise!'

What seemed like a hundred children leapt out from cover, wearing party hats and waving presents. After his first gasp of shock, Gareth was thrilled. He squealed with delight as the other children pressed around him, begging him to open their parcels first. Laura stood rooted to the spot in disbelief and realised that James was smiling triumphantly.

'Did you organise this?' she demanded.

'Yes, I knew you'd been too busy with Bea and Sam to do anything special and I wanted him to have a proper party. What's wrong? Aren't you pleased?'

Laura blinked, trying to come to terms with her own confused feelings. No, to be honest, she wasn't pleased.

Oh, she could see that Gareth was thrilled with all the attention, but that didn't get rid of the gnawing guilt that filled her at the realisation that James had planned this without even knowing that the little boy was his own son. And it didn't help her deal with the prickle of jealousy she felt when the birthday boy launched himself at James and hugged his leg.

'Fank you!' he shouted.

James hugged him back, but his eyes were on Laura. 'What's wrong?' he repeated.

'Nothing,' she choked. 'It was very kind of you. I'll just . . . just go and help in the kitchen.'

Avoiding his gaze, she fled to the kitchen, where she found a smiling young woman in a white chef's outfit up to her eyes in jellies and crisps and sausage rolls. She seemed to have everything under control, and she patted Laura kindly but firmly on the shoulder and urged her to go off and enjoy herself. Since she seemed to have little choice, she went out into the back garden and discovered that a Punch and Judy show was now in progress. She was somewhat comforted when Gareth promptly dragged her into the front row and sat on her lap, but her reprieve didn't last long, since he immediately ordered James to come and join them.

It was almost more than she could bear to see his small hand resting so trustingly on James's large one. As soon as the Punch and Judy show finished, she made an excuse and went back inside, but there was worse to come. Throughout the party she saw that James was in the thick of things—handing out prizes, adjudicating fights and mopping up spilled tomato sauce. If he had been any other man, she would have been warmed by his kindness. As it was, she felt sick to her stomach with anxiety and confusion. Should she tell him the truth, or was it better to let things lie?

Later that evening, when they were alone together, James issued a direct challenge. They had just returned from the hospital and were sitting in front of the living room fire with a decanter of port on the table.

'You're not happy about my organising that party, are you?' he demanded, looking across at her from the depths of his armchair. 'Why not? Did you think I was interfering?'

'I didn't say that.'

He gave a mirthless laugh.

'You didn't have to; it's written all over you. Do you really hate me so much that you don't want me to have any contact with your child?'

Laura drew in breath sharply.

'I didn't say I hated you.'

'It's true, though, isn't it?' he persisted.

His gaze was pitiless, pinning her down so that she felt like a hunted animal transfixed by searchlights.

'All right!' she exclaimed. 'It's true! But don't I have the right to hate you?'

'I would have thought it was the other way round, myself,' he said bitterly. 'That I was the one who had the right to hate you.'

'You arrogant swine!' she exclaimed, rising to her feet and heading for the door. 'Just because I took Bea's place you think you were justified in seducing and abandoning me, don't you?'

He caught up with her and seized her by the shoulders, swinging her round to face him.

'Oh, so that's your version of events, is it? Well, it's odd, but it doesn't bear much resemblance to mine. That stupid little deception of yours had nothing to do with our parting, as you know very well. Except that it should have warned me from the first that you took a delight in deceit and disloyalty.'

'What are you talking about?' she cried indignantly.

'You know very well what I'm talking about! I wasn't your only victim, was I? Not by a long shot! If you don't take a delight in deceit and disloyalty, why didn't you marry that accountant fellow?'

'Because I didn't love him!' shouted Laura.

James paused, shuddering for breath. Then he released her and ran his hands savagely through his hair as if he intended to pull it out by the roots.

'I suppose I can believe that,' he said in a tormented voice. 'But it's a hell of a thing to do to a man who loved you, to run out on him like that. Do you ever see him any more?'

'No,' she replied stormily.

'Never?'

'Never!'

'Then what about Gareth?' he demanded, seizing her shoulders again. 'Are you so vindictive that you won't even let that poor bastard see his own child?'

There was a strange ringing in her ears and her legs felt rubbery and unreliable. She took a deep breath, as if she were poising herself to dive off a high cliff into rock-strewn waters.

'Gareth's not Ray's child,' she whispered. 'He's yours.'

CHAPTER EIGHT

JAMES went white to the lips and his eyes were like burning coals in the stillness of his face.

'Are you sure?'

'Yes.'

'Then why the hell didn't you tell me when you learnt you were pregnant?'

There was bewilderment in his voice, mixed with an unmistakable flare of anger. Laura felt an answering surge of fury. What right did he have to be angry? What right did he have to anything? Even the simple, basic knowledge of his son's existence? She broke away from him and strode across the room, her face working violently as she fought for control.

'After the way you treated me?' she said, swinging around to face him. 'You didn't give me much reason to suppose you would care, did you?'

'After the way I treated you?' said James in a stupefied voice. 'What are you talking about?'

She gave a wild, unsteady laugh.

'I'm talking about the way you used me and discarded me, you brute! It wouldn't have hurt so much if you had admitted right from the start that you only wanted a casual fling, but it was the way you led me on and made me think you cared about me that really upset me. And all the time you were just a lying hypocrite, only after sex without commitment. I'll never forgive you for it!'

James stared at her, aghast.

'I can't believe I'm hearing this. As I see it, I was the injured party, not you.'

'Oh, really? And why do you think that? Because I masqueraded as my sister and hurt your pride?'

'No!' he thundered. 'Because you were engaged to another man when you went to bed with me.'

It was Laura's turn to go white.

'I—I was what?' she stammered.

'You heard me!' he retorted savagely. 'You were engaged to that bloody accountant and you never even had the decency to tell me.'

'Are you out of your mind? I was never engaged to Raymond!'

James gave a vicious laugh.

'That's not what he said!'

'What do you mean?' she cried. 'When did you talk to him?'

'On the day of Sue's party,' he snarled, pacing about the room. 'I came home in turmoil, more than half convinced that I was in love with you and fully intending to go to Sydney with you and find out. I was even wondering whether I was wrong to be so violently opposed to the idea of marrying again. Then I got that rotten phone call.'

Laura stared at him in bewilderment, struggling to absorb what he was telling her. Phrases buzzed in her head—'in love with you...go to Sydney...find out.' Then memories came flashing back from the past. Memories of James sitting in the car, looking at her with passionate urgency, and then the distant shrilling of the telephone and the slam of the car door. Suddenly an ominous sense of misgiving seized her.

'What was that phone call about?' she breathed.

James's eyes leapt with remembered anger.

'I can tell you word for word. God knows, I've gone over it often enough in my mind. There was a man's voice, rather precise. He said, "Good afternoon, my name is Raymond Hall. I believe my fiancée Laura Madison is staying there. May I speak to her, please?" That was all.'

Laura felt as sick as if someone had punched her in the stomach. She leaned against the door for support as the full implication of this revelation struck her.

'So you thought I was engaged to Ray and that I had gone to bed with you just for the fun of it?' she demanded in a dazed voice.

'What else was I supposed to think?'

'Well, what did you do? Did you question him about it?'

'No! I simply said, I don't know where she is, and hung up. I was half out of my mind with shock. If he'd been there in person, I probably would have knocked him down.'

'Instead of which, you did the emotional equivalent to me,' cried Laura fiercely. 'You told me the game was over and it was time to call it quits. That was cruel, James. It was heartless and selfish and cruel!'

'Well, didn't I have the right to be cruel after what you'd done to me?'

'No, you didn't!' she shouted, her anger blazing up to match his. 'You had no right whatsoever, because I was never engaged to Raymond Hall—as you would have found out if you'd only bothered to ask me. What he told you was pure rubbish!'

A stunned silence descended on the room, so that the only sound was the hiss of a log breaking and falling into the embers amid a shower of orange sparks. Then James took a sharp, unsteady breath.

'Come off it!' he snarled. 'Why would he say he was engaged to you if he wasn't?'

'Because he's a pompous idiot who thinks he only has to issue orders and the world jumps to obey them!'

'Well, there must have been something between you to make him say that,' muttered James.

'There was something between us,' she agreed bitterly. 'A giant communication failure! Raymond asked me to marry him just before I came down to Tasmania to take Bea's place. I thought about it, but I knew it would never work so I rang him from here and said no. He didn't seem to get the message, so when I went back to Sydney I said no again. He was simply too conceited to believe me.'

'Were you sleeping with him?' demanded James.

Laura's mouth contorted.

'I don't see that it's any business of yours now, but no, I wasn't! I didn't realise he thought of me as anything more than a friend till he popped the question, but I could never have married him. There was no special spark between us.'

James swore violently under his breath and suddenly covered his eyes with his hand.

'I can't believe what a fool I've been,' he said in a tormented voice. 'Do you really mean there was nothing between you?'

'Nothing,' confirmed Laura.

'And I drove you away...' His voice thickened with remorse, and suddenly he caught her in his arms. 'Laura, there are no words strong enough to express what I feel, but I have to try anyway. I'm hot-headed and I jumped to conclusions. I should have known you would never do anything so underhanded—I should have trusted you. I'm sorry—deeply sorry. Can you ever forgive me?'

She could feel the wild beating of his heart, the warmth of his body coming off him in waves, the power in those strongly bunched muscles that encircled her like steel cables. For a moment she felt an overwhelming impulse simply to burrow into his chest and cling to him, murmuring the words that he wanted to hear. After all, his explanation had flowed into her wounded heart like a healing balm, soothing her hurt pride and restoring her self-esteem.

It hadn't just been a game with him! He had been genuinely attracted to her, had wanted their relationship to continue. But there was more at stake here than just her dignity. There was her whole future and Gareth's too. With a pang of insight she realised how fatally easy it would be to slip back into a passionate affair with James without resolving anything. A spasm crossed her face and she looked up at him bleakly.

'I don't know,' she choked. 'I simply don't know, James.'

He heaved a deep sigh and nodded.

'That's fair enough. Why should you forgive me, just because I leapt to conclusions that any sane man would have resisted? All I had to do was swallow my pride nearly three years ago and ask a few questions and I could have avoided this heartache that I've put us both through. I probably don't even have the right to ask you this, Laura, but was it true what you told me at Sue's party? Were you in love with me then?'

She didn't trust herself to speak, so she simply caught her upper lip in her teeth and nodded.

James's eyes kindled.

'You were always brave, Laura. You had the courage to admit what you felt right from the start, but I didn't— even to myself. I found out after you'd gone, though.

You see, I missed you unbearably. Hated you. Wanted you. Loved you. I never stopped loving you, even when I thought you were married to someone else.'

She had to swallow hard and clear her throat before she could speak.

'Then why didn't you ring me in Sydney and tell me?'

'Because I believed you'd made your choice, and I couldn't face the humiliation of hearing your husband answer the phone.'

'Didn't Bea tell you that I wasn't married?'

'No. Bea seems to have taken some kind of vow of silence about you. She's never mentioned anything to do with you.'

Laura smiled wryly.

'That was my doing. I made her promise not to discuss me with you. Ever. I never told her why, but I think she suspects.'

They were both silent for a moment, busy with their own thoughts. Then James spoke curtly.

'And you haven't met anyone else since Gareth was born? Anyone you would consider marrying?'

Laura shook her head.

'No.' She wanted to ask him the same question, but prudence restrained her. She wasn't at all sure where they were going from here, and she didn't want James to think that he would only have to snap his fingers and she would come running back to him. She must remain calm and detached, but it wasn't easy when James's eyes were gazing at her so intently.

'Neither have I,' he said hoarsely. 'Once I lost you, I also lost interest in any other women. I knew that nobody else could compare with you.'

Laura forgot about trying to be detached.

'Sue—' she began with difficulty.

'There was never anything between Sue and me, except pity on my side and desperation on hers. Sue's husband Jack had a drinking problem and was violent towards her. I felt sorry for her and listened when she wanted to talk. For a while she transferred all her confused emotions onto me and convinced herself she was in love with me, but it wasn't true and she eventually realised it herself.'

'That night you went down to visit her you stayed away for two and a half hours,' said Laura sceptically. 'And your hair was wet when you came back, as if you'd been in the shower.'

'I had been in the shower! She had a broken pipe that was leaking under the house and I offered to have a look at it for her. I had to crawl around under the floorboards and I got filthy.'

'Oh,' said Laura in a small voice. Then another thought struck her. 'What about the way your sister Wendy always said you were such a playboy, pursuing women but never getting seriously involved with them?'

James grimaced.

'There's a certain amount of truth in that,' he admitted. 'After my wife Paula left me, I was very bitter about women in general.'

'Why?' asked Laura. 'What did she do to you?'

'It's a long story. I was only nineteen when I met her and I fell passionately in love with her. Or thought I did. I realise now with hindsight that we had nothing in common but sex. The whole thing would probably have petered out if she hadn't told me after a couple of months that she was pregnant.'

Laura flinched. This was the first time she had ever had any inkling that James might have another child somewhere, and she could not deny that the thought gave her pain. At the same time she felt a rush of sympathy for the other young woman, who must have experienced similar heartache to her.

'Poor girl,' she said. 'How old was she?'

'Twenty-one.'

'And you were only nineteen? That's a big age difference at that point. But you were both terribly young to cope with being parents.'

'We didn't cope with being parents,' said James harshly. 'We didn't become parents.'

'You mean she had an abor—'

'No! Look, when she told me she was pregnant, I was over the moon. I was so thrilled at the thought of being a father, so proud of her, so anxious to do the right thing. I told her immediately that we'd get married and she seemed as happy about it as I was. But my father hit the roof when he heard the news.'

'What happened?' asked Laura.

'I had been on the point of heading off to Harvard to do a commerce degree and he threatened that if I married Paula he would withdraw all financial support.'

'What did you do?'

'I told him to stuff his financial support and married her anyway. Then I got a job as a deckhand on a fishing boat so that I could support her.'

'What went wrong between you?' demanded Laura.

James gave a savage laugh.

'The first thing was that she admitted that she had never been pregnant. It was only a story she had made up so that I would marry her. My father was the wealthiest farmer in the area, and she knew about my plans for going to the United States, so she thought I'd be her ticket to a wider and more interesting world. When she found that I'd quarrelled with him and wasn't going to get any money, she was furious with me. She told me flatly that she didn't intend to spend the rest of her life mouldering away in a fishing village and either I had to find some way of supporting her or the marriage was over.'

'So what did you do?' asked Laura.

'I was pretty stunned, but I begged her to give the marriage a chance. I didn't have any particular skills at that stage but I was making good money on the fishing boat. I promised her that if she'd just stick it out for another three years or so, while I got some savings together, we'd go to America and I'd open some kind of business there.'

'But that didn't happen?'

James's mouth set in a grim line.

'No, it didn't. Paula managed to arrange her passage to America a bit faster than that. About two years after we were married I came back early from a fishing trip and found her in bed with a hotshot American investor who'd come out to visit one of the scallop farms here. I'd had my suspicions for some time that she was being unfaithful to me, and in a way it was almost a relief to have it out in the open. We agreed to get a divorce and she went off to America with him and later married him.'

'How did you feel about it?' asked Laura hesitantly.

He shrugged.

'Devastated at first, but that was mainly hurt pride. Once I got used to the idea I was glad the marriage was over, because we'd done nothing but make each other unhappy for the entire two years it lasted. The whole thing was a disaster, and the worst part about it was that it coloured my view of women for years afterwards.'

'Is that why you're so down on deceit and disloyalty?'

James smiled wryly.

'Yes, but I took precautions to protect myself from then on. It seems ridiculous to me now, but I was so determined not to get caught again that I avoided the kind of women I might have fallen genuinely in love with. Instead I had a lot of shallow, meaningless affairs with shallow, meaningless women. Until I met you.'

Laura was more touched by this blunt admission than she wanted him to guess. She tried to cover her emotion with a show of scepticism.

'And then?' she prompted brusquely.

James put up his hand and massaged his temple as if he had a headache.

'And then I knew I was in big trouble,' he admitted. 'From the first moment I saw you, here in this very house, I was immediately intrigued by you. I had come along, simmering with prejudice and determined to dislike you, because I thought you were going to be another woman like Paula. Only out to marry Sam for your own advantage and not really caring a damn about him. But you were so different from what I expected. In spite of those weird clothes you were wearing, you really seemed to have genuine dignity and character. It was even worse when I took you to that wedding rehearsal and had to pretend I was marrying you. I couldn't help but wonder what it would be like if it were really true, and I was appalled to discover that I was very powerfully attracted to you.'

'It was exactly the same for me,' broke in Laura, abandoning all pretence of detachment.

He gritted his teeth and sighed.

'I thought as much,' he said. 'But I swear that when I took you out on that beach I had no intention of doing anything except trying to persuade you not to marry Sam. I thought it would be a mistake for both of you if you rushed into it. Then, before I knew it, I had you in my arms and I was kissing you as I've never kissed any woman in my life. It felt like the best and worst deed I'd ever done. It was so right, so natural, so good to hold you like that, and yet I believed you were my nephew's fiancée. I couldn't believe I was capable of such treachery, so I dealt with my anger by blaming you for it. I told myself you *were* another woman like Paula, getting married just for your own advantage with no intention of making it work.'

Laura made a sound that was halfway between a groan and a laugh.

'You must have got an awful shock on Bea's wedding day when you discovered who I really was,' she said.

James's eyes flashed murderously at the recollection.

'Calling it a shock is the understatement of the century,' he said. 'At first I was too stunned to take it in, but then I felt the most incredible relief. You weren't going to marry someone else, you were still free, which meant that I had a chance with you. But then I started to think about how you'd made a complete fool of me, and I could have tanned your hide.'

Laura flashed him a guilty smile.

'It wasn't a very good beginning, was it?' she muttered.

To her surprise, James suddenly cupped her face in his hands and gazed earnestly down at her.

'Yes, it was,' he insisted. 'Any beginning with you would have been a good beginning, because the only thing that matters is that we found each other. I've been a fool, Laura. I treated you badly and I let my arrogance and hurt pride about the past erect barriers between us which should never have been there. But I am sure of one thing now.'

'What's that?' she asked shakily.

'That I love you, and I'm never going to stop loving you. Laura, I probably don't have the right to ask you this, but will you please, please marry me?'

She was filled by a rush of emotion which threatened to sweep her off her feet, an intoxicating mixture of joy and sadness, pain and regret, anger and forgiveness and a bright, shining hope. Even now she struggled to be cautious.

'Are you asking me just because of Gareth?' she demanded.

James swore softly under his breath.

'No, I'm not asking you because of Gareth,' he said. 'He's a great little guy, and I'm already beginning to love him, but that's not the reason I'm asking you to marry me. I'm asking because I love you, because I can't imagine how I'll live without you. I've spent the last three years making you miserable and now I'd like to spend the rest of my life making you happy. Will you let me try?'

Laura looked up at those tawny gold eyes fixed intently on her, at the urgent, troubled set of his mouth and made her decision. Hadn't she once told him that you had to be prepared to take risks when you fell in love? Except that this time she didn't feel that she was taking a risk. Now for the first time she felt absolutely certain that she could trust James for the rest of her life. Twining her arms around his neck, she stood on tiptoe and kissed him fiercely on the lips.

'Yes,' she said.

With a groan of triumph he caught her against him, crushing her so hard that he squeezed the breath out of her.

'Do you know what I'm going to do to you?' he demanded huskily.

A tremor went through her.

'Oh, I think I can take a wild guess,' she murmured, moistening her lower lip with her tongue.

'You shameless little hussy,' he breathed admiringly, pressing his lips against the pulse that beat in her throat. 'Tell me, then.'

She lifted her open mouth and whispered in his ear, enjoying the sudden flare of excitement in his eyes as he strained to catch the soft, tickling words.

'Does that appeal to you?' she finished demurely.

'It will do for starters,' he growled. 'And after that I'm going to—'

A hot rush of arousal throbbed through her as he told her in vivid, shameless detail exactly what he planned for her. And, while he was talking, he was busy calmly unbuttoning her silk blouse and peeling off her tights and knickers.

'Unfair,' she whispered. 'You're still fully dressed.'

'I won't be for long. And I want you ready for what I'm planning.' His warm fingers stroked up the inside of her thigh and then slid teasingly inside her, so that she shuddered and clamped her teeth down on a soft moan.

'Well, what a pleasant surprise. So you are ready? Good. But you're going to be more than ready by the time I take you, my darling. You're going to be whimpering and crying out and writhing in my arms and wanting this more than you've ever wanted anything in your life. Aren't you?'

A pang of pure, unfulfilled need lanced through her at those hoarse, seductive words. When his hands brushed over her breasts, caressing their aching fullness, she strained against him, offering her open, trembling lips to him.

'Yes,' she breathed.

Cupping her face in his hands, he bent her backwards and kissed her with a deep, savage hunger that made the blood roar in her ears. Only when he had plundered her mouth again and again did he suddenly sweep her off the floor and gaze down at her, his breath coming in long, heaving gulps.

'You drive me insane with longing, Laura,' he growled. 'Night after night since we parted I've dreamed of doing this to you. Well, now I'm not going to wait any longer. Once I make you mine, nothing will ever part us again.'

With a sharp, indrawn breath he wrenched open the door and strode swiftly down the hall, carrying her as effortlessly as if she were weightless. The gold-striped wallpaper and antique paintings spun past her and then she heard the creak of James's bedroom door as it opened. Once inside he kicked it shut and turned the heavy key in the lock.

'Is Gareth given to night-time wandering?' he asked.

She shook her head.

'Good, because I have a very long night planned for you.'

Striding across to the bed, he set her down in the middle of it, switched on the bedside lamp and sat beside her, gazing hungrily down at her. Then his face clouded.

'What is it?' she asked in a troubled voice, reaching up to touch his cheek.

He turned his head and kissed the plump cushion of flesh at the base of her thumb.

'I'm afraid you'll get pregnant, and I've no protection to offer you at this moment. We can wait if you want to, and I'll go to a pharmacy tomorrow.'

She shook her head, relieved that that was the only thing troubling him. For a moment she had feared that he had changed his mind about everything he had just told her.

'No,' she said with passionate certainty. 'I don't want to wait. And anyway, I'm not likely to become pregnant at the moment.'

'But what if it does happen?' he persisted, stroking her tumbled hair with a tormented expression. 'There's nothing I'd like better myself than to give you another baby. It thrills me to the core even to think of it, and this time I'd be there to help you through it all, but if you don't want to take the risk—'

'I do want to!' she insisted. 'And if we don't make a baby tonight, then I want to do it soon, James, very soon. I love you and I want your children. I can't tell you how much.'

'Oh, sweetheart.' He gathered her in his arms and held her with crushing force. All the things they wanted to say seemed to flow between them without words, then gradually the nature of their embrace began to change. His hands moved over her satiny skin and he stroked her naked body until she could bear it no longer.

'Are you going to get undressed, or aren't you?' she demanded impatiently.

He looked down at her with a slow, sultry smile that made something melt inside her.

'That's an invitation I can't refuse. If you're going to be a good wife, you'll have to learn to do certain things for me. You can start by unbuckling my belt and seeing what you can find there. Go on, do as you're told.'

A hot flood of colour rushed to her cheeks, but with trembling fingers she obeyed. The heavy leather and brass seemed to jam obstinately, but with a sharp tug she worked the belt free from the buckle, then slowly, tauntingly, unzipped his jeans. A soft gasp escaped her as she saw the powerful ridge outlined beneath his jockey shorts. All she could think of was how much she wanted to touch it, rub herself against it, feel its heat and hardness deep inside her. Hesitantly she ran her hand down over it, then more daringly slipped her fingers inside his underwear and gripped him hard. James gave a low groan.

'I think I've died and gone to heaven. Laura, if you're serious about loving and marrying me, will you please rip off my clothes so that I can have you? Now!'

With a muffled giggle she lay naked on top of him and began half-heartedly fumbling with his shirt buttons. But, since most of her efforts were directed to kissing his eyelids and brushing her naked breasts against his face, he soon became impatient with her progress. Letting out a low, animal roar he sat up, flung her on her back and began tearing off his clothes himself.

'If you're trying to drive me out of my mind, you've succeeded,' he growled, hauling his shirt over his head and flinging it into a corner of the room, followed by a volley of other garments. 'And you've only yourself to blame for the consequences.'

Trapping her against the pillows, he began to kiss her, and lowered the full weight of his body onto her, so that she was crushed pleasurably beneath him. His tongue thrust into her mouth and she felt an answering rush of heat deep inside her. Arching her back, she thrust herself against him, so that she felt his male hardness stir and throb against her. She cried out as his fingers skimmed down between her thighs, parting her softness so that he could bring her to the point of frenzy with his touch.

In the soft glow of the lamplight she could see him watching her from under half-closed lids, and when her breathing quickened into a gasping, staccato rhythm he

suddenly reared up and crouched over her, his face dark
and distorted with need.

'I can't wait another moment,' he breathed. 'I want
to be deep inside you, Laura.'

Groping with his hand, he lodged his virile hardness
against her and plunged in. A cry broke from her lips
at the explosive, sundering force of that invasion and
yet she gloried in it, taking delight in his size and power
and ruthless energy. The ache that filled her was wholly
pleasurable and she strained to meet him at each thrust,
threshing her head from side to side and moaning as he
found her innermost depths. A strange sensation kept
building and building inside her, with the unstoppable
force of an ocean wave, gathering strength until at last
it broke and shattered with immeasurable force, leaving
her gasping in total fulfilment.

'I—love—you, James,' she whispered.

He went on ruthlessly pounding away at her, his face
intent and strange, as if he were absorbed in some eerie
trance, until at last he, too, stiffened and cried out. The
warm gush of his climax filled her and his arms tightened
around her.

'I love you too, Laura,' he breathed.

As he buried his face in her neck and his frantic
breathing slowed she felt his lips press warmly against
her throat, and a joyful sense of complete happiness
flowed through her.

'When can we get married?' she asked, hugging him
hard.

'Tomorrow morning.'

'No. Seriously.'

'The moment I can book the church and arrange a
licence. I want you as my wife, Laura, and I don't intend
to wait.'

*   *   *

It was a perfect day for a wedding, so bright and sunny that it was impossible to believe that it was still only late winter. A pink, frothy blossom covered the cherry trees in the rectory garden next door to the church and drifts of daffodils tossed their heads beneath the bare oak trees. Here and there a few sheep had escaped from a nearby paddock and wandered around nibbling the grass that grew in lush clumps around the weathered gravestones.

All of this Laura noticed as she arrived, flustered and breathless, ten minutes late for her own wedding. It was so unlike her to be late that James had grown worried and come out of the church into the porch to look out for her. Hastily she wrenched open the car door and jumped out, waving her bouquet of scented frangipani.

'James, I'm here!' she called.

He strode across to meet her and stood looking down at her, his tawny eyes glowing warmly.

'I was afraid you'd changed your mind,' he teased.

'It wasn't that! I couldn't get my hair to sit properly and then I laddered my tights and—oh, James, do I look all right?'

His gaze took in every detail, from the little wreath of flowers in her hair down to her ivory-coloured tailored silk dress and pearl drop earrings.

'You look gorgeous,' he told her approvingly.

At that moment Bea came limping across from the porch in her red attendant's frock and grinned at them both, her dark eyes dancing.

'All ready to go?' she asked. 'Sam's inside getting restless.'

Laura's eyes twinkled too as she remembered the last time they had met for a wedding in this very spot.

'Now that we're all here, I suppose that we should introduce ourselves,' she said. 'I'm Laura, she's Bea, you must be James. I'm the bride, she's the bridesmaid, you're marrying me. Now, let's get started, shall we?'

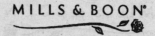

MILLS & BOON®

Next Month's Romances

♡

Each month you can choose from a wide variety of romance novels from Mills & Boon. Below are the new titles to look out for next month from the Presents and Enchanted series.

Presents™

WICKED CAPRICE	Anne Mather
A LESSON IN SEDUCTION	Susan Napier
MADDIE'S LOVE-CHILD	Miranda Lee
A HUSBAND'S REVENGE	Lee Wilkinson
MARRIAGE-SHY	Karen van der Zee
HERS FOR A NIGHT	Kate Walker
A WIFE OF CONVENIENCE	Kim Lawrence
THE PLAYBOY	Catherine O'Connor

Enchanted™

LIVING NEXT DOOR TO ALEX	Catherine George
ENDING IN MARRIAGE	Debbie Macomber
SOPHIE'S SECRET	Anne Weale
VALENTINE, TEXAS	Kate Denton
THE BRIDE, THE BABY AND THE BEST MAN	
	Liz Fielding
A CONVENIENT BRIDE	Angela Wells
TO LASSO A LADY	Renee Roszel
TO LOVE THEM ALL	Eva Rutland

FREE!

FOUR FREE
specially selected
Presents™ novels
PLUS a Mystery Gift
when you return this card...

Return this coupon and we'll send you 4 Mills & Boon® Presents™ novels and a mystery gift absolutely FREE! We'll even pay the postage and packing for you.

We're making you this offer to introduce you to the benefits of the Reader Service™– FREE home delivery of brand-new Mills & Boon Presents novels, at least a month before they are available in the shops, FREE gifts and a monthly Newsletter packed with information.

Accepting these FREE books and gift places you under no obligation to buy, you may cancel at any time, even after receiving just your free shipment. Simply complete the coupon below and send it to:

MILLS & BOON READER SERVICE, FREEPOST, CROYDON, SURREY, CR9 3WZ.

No stamp needed

Yes, please send me 4 free Presents novels and a mystery gift. I understand that unless you hear from me, I will receive 6 superb new titles every month for just £2.10* each, postage and packing free. I am under no obligation to purchase any books and I may cancel or suspend my subscription at any time, but the free books and gift will be mine to keep in any case. (I am over 18 years of age)

P7XE

Ms/Mrs/Miss/Mr _____

Address _____

_____

_____ Postcode _____

MILLS & BOON®

By Request

Bestselling romances brought back to you by popular demand

◆

Two complete novels in one volume by bestselling author

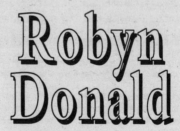

Robyn Donald

Paradise Lost

Pagan Surrender

Available: February 1997   Price: £4.50